WE IMAGINE OURSELVES

WE IMAGINE OURSELVES

A Science Fiction
Anthology

Cover Illustration Raelyn

Background

Science fiction started to mature as a genre in the early nineteenth century with books such as Mary Shelley's *Frankenstein* and Edgar Allan Poe's *The Unparalleled Adventure of One Hans Pfaall*. H.G. Wells and Jules Verne began to publish their works inspired by new technologies later in the century, termed "scientific romance" at that time.

Pulp magazines like Amazing Stories appeared in the early twentieth century and helped to popularize the genre. Amazing Stories was published in 1926 and featured such writers as Isaac Asimov and Frederik Pohl. The market for science fiction flourished; but World War II brought paper shortages, and the market didn't begin to recover until the 1940s.

Galaxy Science Fiction was an American sci fi magazine published 1950-1980. Many notable science fiction authors had stories published in this literary magazine, including "The Fireman," which Ray Bradbury would later expand and publish as Fahrenheit 451. The magazine was a major influencer on since fiction in its heyday.

The stories in this anthology were published in Galaxy Science Fiction in the 1950s.

~ ~ ~

In this Workman Classic Schoolbooks anthology, spellings have been standardized to modern American and a few errors in the text have been corrected. No attempt has been made to modernize or dumb down the original language. Most words can be understood in context, but if you're not sure, look them up. Less common words have been included in the vocabulary exercises. Of course, being science fiction, some words are made up!

Enjoy your read!

P.D. Workman

Table of Contents

WHAT IS POSAT?

By PHYLLIS STERLING SMITH
Illustrated by ED ALEXANDER

Of course coming events cast their shadows before, but this shadow was 400 years long!

The following advertisement appeared in the July 1953 issue of several magazines:

MASTERY OF ALL KNOWLEDGE CAN BE YOURS!
What is the secret source of those
Profound principles that can solve the problems of life?
Send for our FREE booklet of explanation.
Do not be a leaf in the wind! YOU can alter the course of your life!
Tap the treasury of Wisdom through the ages!
The Perpetual Order of Seekers After Truth
POSAT
an ancient secret society

Most readers passed it by with scarcely a glance. It was, after all, similar to the many that had appeared through the years under the name of that same society. Other readers, as their eyes slid over the familiar format of the ad, speculated idly about the persistent and mildly mysterious organization behind it. A few even resolved to clip the attached coupon and send for the booklet—sometime—when a pen or pencil was nearer at hand.

Bill Evans, an unemployed pharmacist, saw the ad in a copy of *Your Life and Psychology* that had been abandoned on his seat in the bus. He filled out the blanks on the coupon with a scrap of stubby pencil. "You can alter the course of your life!" he read again. He particularly liked that thought, even though he had long since ceased to believe it. He actually took the trouble to mail the coupon. After all, he had, literally, nothing to lose, and nothing else to occupy his time.

Miss Elizabeth Arnable was one of the few to whom the advertisement was unfamiliar. As a matter of fact, she very seldom read a magazine. The radio in her room took the place of reading matter, and she always liked to think that it amused her cats as well as herself. Reading would be so selfish under the circumstances, wouldn't it? Not but what the cats weren't almost smart enough to read, she always said.

It just so happened, however, that she had bought a copy of the *Antivivisectionist Gazette* the day before. She pounced upon the POSAT ad as a trout might snap at a particularly attractive fly. Having filled out the coupon with violet ink, she invented an errand that would take her past the neighborhood post office so that she could post it as soon as possible.

Donald Alford, research physicist, came across the POSAT ad tucked at the bottom of a column in *The Bulletin of Physical Research*. He was engrossed in the latest paper by Dr. Crandon, a man whom he admired from the point of view of both a former student and a fellow research worker. Consequently, he was one of the many who passed over the POSAT ad with the disregard accorded to any common object.

He read with interest to the end of the article before he realized that some component of the advertisement had been noted by a region of his brain just beyond consciousness. It teased at him like a tickle that couldn't be scratched until he turned back to the page.

It was the symbol or emblem of POSAT, he realized, that had caught his attention. The perpendicularly crossed ellipses centered with a small black circle might almost be a conventionalized version of the Bohr atom of helium. He smiled with mild skepticism as he read through the printed matter that accompanied it.

"I wonder what their racket is," he mused. Then, because his typewriter was conveniently at hand, he carefully tore out the coupon and inserted it in the machine. The spacing of the typewriter didn't fit the dotted lines on the coupon, of course, but he didn't bother to correct it. He addressed an envelope, laid it with other mail to be posted, and promptly forgot all about it. Since he was a methodical man, it was entrusted to the U.S. mail early the next morning, together with his other letters.

Three identical forms accompanied the booklet which POSAT sent in response to the three inquiries. The booklet gave no more information than had the original advertisement, but with considerable more volubility. It promised the recipient the secrets of the Cosmos and the key that would unlock the hidden knowledge within himself—if he would merely fill out the enclosed form.

Bill Evans, the unemployed pharmacist, let the paper lie unanswered for several days. To be quite honest, he was disappointed. Although he had mentally disclaimed all belief in anything that POSAT might offer, he had watched the return mails with anticipation. His own resources were almost at an end, and he had reached the point where intervention by something supernatural, or at least superhuman, seemed the only hope.

He had hoped, unreasonably, that POSAT had an answer. But time lay heavily upon him, and he used it one evening to write the requested information—about his employment (ha!), his religious beliefs, his reason for inquiring about POSAT, his financial situation. Without quite knowing that he did so, he communicated in his terse answers some of his desperation and sense of futility.

Miss Arnable was delighted with the opportunity for autobiographical composition. It required five extra sheets of paper to convey all the information that she wished to give—all about her poor, dear father who had been a missionary to China, and the kinship that she felt toward the mystic cults of the East, her belief that her cats were reincarnations of her loved ones (which, she stated, derived from a religion of the Persians; or was it the Egyptians?) and in her complete and absolute acceptance of everything that POSAT had stated in their booklet. And what would the dues be? She wished to join immediately. Fortunately, dear father had left her in a comfortable financial situation.

To Donald Alford, the booklet seemed to confirm his suspicion that POSAT was a racket of some sort. Why else would they be interested in his employment or financial position? It also served to increase his curiosity.

"What do you suppose they're driving at?" he asked his wife Betty, handing her the booklet and questionnaire.

"I don't really know what to say," she answered, squinting a little as she usually did when puzzled. "I know one thing, though, and that's that you won't stop until you find out!"

"The scientific attitude," he acknowledged with a grin.

"Why don't you fill out this questionnaire incognito, though?" she suggested. "Pretend that we're wealthy and see if they try to get our money. Do they have anything yet except your name and address?"

Don was shocked. "If I send this back to them, it will have to be with correct answers!"

"The scientific attitude again," Betty sighed. "Don't you ever let your imagination run away with the facts a bit? What are you going to give for your reasons for asking about POSAT?"

"Curiosity," he replied, and, pulling his fountain pen from his vest pocket, he wrote exactly that, in small, neat script.

It was unfortunate for his curiosity that Don could not see the contents of the three envelopes that were mailed from the offices of POSAT the following week. For this time they differed.

Bill Evans was once again disappointed. The pamphlet that was enclosed gave what apparently meant to be final answers to life's problems. They were couched in vaguely metaphysical terms and offered absolutely no help to him.

His disappointment was tempered, however, by the knowledge that he had unexpectedly found a job. Or, rather, it had fallen into his lap. When he had thought that every avenue of employment had been tried, a position had been offered him in a wholesale pharmacy in the older industrial part of the city. It was not a particularly attractive place to work, located as it was next to a large warehouse, but to him it was hope for the future.

It amused him to discover that the offices of POSAT were located on the other side of the same warehouse, at the end of a blind alley. Blind alley indeed! He felt vaguely ashamed for having placed any confidence in them.

Miss Arnable was thrilled to discover that her envelope contained not only several pamphlets, (she scanned the titles rapidly and found that one of them concerned the sacred cats of ancient Egypt), but that it contained also a small pin with the symbol of POSAT wrought in gold and black enamel. The covering letter said that she had been accepted as an active member of POSAT and that the dues were five dollars per month; please remit by return mail. She wrote a check immediately, and settled contentedly into a chair to peruse the article on sacred cats.

After a while she began to read aloud so that her own cats could enjoy it, too.

Don Alford would not have been surprised if his envelope had shown contents similar to the ones that the others received. The folded sheets of paper that he pulled forth, however, made him stiffen with sharp surprise.

• • •

Vocabulary words:
Find these words in the section, write the sentence they are used in, and write your own definition. If you are stuck, look it up in the dictionary, but still write a definition in your own words.

antivivisectionist
perpendicularly
incognito
metaphysical

Comprehension/extension questions:

What do you suppose has surprised Don Alford?

WHAT IS POSAT?

Is it a coincidence that Bill Evans has found a job?

What do you think POSAT is up to?

• • •

"Come here a minute, Betty," he called, spreading them out carefully on the dining room table. "What do you make of these?"

She came, dishcloth in hand, and thoughtfully examined them, one by one. "Multiple choice questions! It looks like a psychological test of some sort."

"This isn't the kind of thing I expected them to send me," worried Don. "Look at the type of thing they ask. 'If you had discovered a new and virulent poison that could be compounded from common household ingredients, would you (1) publish the information in a daily newspaper, (2) manufacture it secretly and sell it as rodent exterminator, (3) give the information to the armed forces for use as a secret weapon, or (4) withhold the information entirely as too dangerous to be passed on?'"

"Could they be a spy ring?" asked Betty. "Subversive agents? Anxious to find out your scientific secrets like that classified stuff that you're so careful of when you bring it home from the lab?"

Don scanned the papers quickly. "There's nothing here that looks like an attempt to get information. Besides, I've told them nothing about my work except that I do research in physics. They don't even know what company I work for. If this is a psychological test, it measures attitudes, nothing else. Why should they want to know my attitudes?"

"Do you suppose that POSAT is really what it claims to be—a secret society—and that they actually screen their applicants?"

He smiled wryly. "Wouldn't it be interesting if I didn't make the grade after starting out to expose their racket?"

He pulled out his pen and sat down to the task of resolving the dilemmas before him.

His next communication from POSAT came to his business address and, paradoxically, was more personal than its forerunners.

Dear Doctor Alford:

We have examined with interest the information that you have sent to us. We are happy to inform you that, thus far, you have satisfied the requirements for membership in the Perpetual Order of Seekers After Truth. Before accepting new members into this ancient and honorable secret society, we find it desirable that they have a personal interview with the Grand Chairman of POSAT.

Accordingly, you are cordially invited to an audience with our Grand Chairman on Tuesday, July 10, at 2:30 P.M. Please let us know if this arrangement is acceptable to you. If not, we will attempt to make another appointment for you.

The time specified for the appointment was hardly a convenient one for Don. At 2:30 P.M. on most Tuesdays, he would be at work in the laboratory. And while his employers made no complaint if he took his research problems home with him and worried over them half the night, they were not equally enthusiastic when he used working hours for pursuing unrelated interests. Moreover, the headquarters of POSAT was in a town almost a hundred miles distant. Could he afford to take a whole day off for chasing will-o-wisps?

It hardly seemed worth the trouble. He wondered if Betty would be disappointed if he dropped the whole matter. Since the letter had been sent to the laboratory instead of his home, he couldn't consult her about it without telephoning.

Since the letter had been sent to the laboratory instead of his home! But it was impossible!

He searched feverishly through his pile of daily mail for the envelope in which the letter had come. The address stared up at him, unmistakably and fearfully legible. The name of his company. The number of the room he worked in. In short, the address that he had never given them!

"Get hold of yourself," he commanded his frightened mind. "There's some perfectly logical, easy explanation for this. They looked it up in the directory of the Institute of Physics. Or in the alumni directory of the university. Or—or—"

But the more he thought about it, the more sinister it seemed. His laboratory address was available, but why should POSAT take the trouble of looking it up? Some prudent impulse had led him to withhold that particular bit of information, yet now, for some reason of their own, POSAT had unearthed the information.

His wife's words echoed in his mind, "Could they be a spy ring? Subversive agents?"

Don shook his head as though to clear away the confusion. His conservative habit of thought made him reject that explanation as too melodramatic.

At least one decision was easier to reach because of his doubts. Now he knew he had to keep his appointment with the Grand Chairman of POSAT.

He scribbled a memo to the department office stating that he would not be at work on Tuesday.

• • •

Vocabulary words:
Find these words in the section, write the sentence they are used in, and write your own definition. If you are stuck, look it up in the dictionary, but still write a definition in your own words.

compounded
paradoxically
subversive
will-o-wisps

Comprehension/extension questions:

What was it that surprised Alford about the letter?

Why doesn't he believe his wife's explanation?

WHAT IS POSAT?

• • •

At first Don Alford had some trouble locating the POSAT headquarters. It seemed to him that the block in which the street number would fall was occupied entirely by a huge sprawling warehouse, of concrete construction, and almost entirely windowless. It was recessed from the street in several places to make room for the small, shabby buildings of a wholesale pharmacy, a printer's plant, an upholstering shop, and was also indented by alleys lined with loading platforms.

It was at the back of one of the alleys that he finally found a door marked with the now familiar emblem of POSAT.

He opened the frosted glass door with a feeling of misgiving, and faced a dark flight of stairs leading to the upper floor. Somewhere above him a buzzer sounded, evidently indicating his arrival. He picked his way up through the murky stairwell.

The reception room was hardly a cheerful place, with its battered desk facing the view of the empty alley, and a film of dust obscuring the pattern of the gray-looking wallpaper and worn rug. But the light of the summer afternoon filtering through the window scattered the gloom somewhat, enough to help Don doubt that he would find the menace here that he had come to expect.

The girl addressing envelopes at the desk looked very ordinary. *Not the Mata-Hari*[1] *type*, thought Don, with an inward chuckle at his own suspicions. He handed her the letter.

She smiled. "We've been expecting you, Dr. Alford. If you'll just step into the next room——"

She opened a door opposite the stairwell, and Don stepped through it.

The sight of the luxurious room before him struck his eyes with the shock of a dentist's drill, so great was the contrast between it and the shabby reception room. For a moment Don had difficulty breathing. The rug—Don had seen one like it before, but it had been in a museum. The paintings on the walls, ornately framed in gilt carving, were surely old masters—of the Renaissance period, he guessed. Although he recognized none of the pictures, he felt that he could almost name the artists. That glowing one near the corner would probably be a Titian. Or was it Tintorretto? He regretted for a moment the lost opportunities of his college days, when he had passed up Art History in favor of Operational Circuit Analysis.

The girl opened a filing cabinet, the front of which was set flush with the wall, and, selecting a folder from it, disappeared through another door.

Don sprang to examine the picture near the corner. It was hung at eye level—that is, at the eye level of the

------

[1] Margaretha Zelle, a performer convicted of being a German spy in World War I.

average person. Don had to bend over a bit to see it properly. He searched for a signature. Apparently there was none. But did artists sign their pictures back in those days? He wished he knew more about such things.

Each of the paintings was individually lighted by a fluorescent tube held on brackets directly above it. As Don straightened up from his scrutiny of the picture, he inadvertently hit his head against the light. The tube, dislodged from its brackets, fell to the rug with a muffled thud.

Now I've done it! thought Don with dismay. But at least the tube hadn't shattered.

In fact—it was still glowing brightly! His eyes registered the fact, even while his mind refused to believe it. He raised his eyes to the brackets. They were simple pieces of solid hardware designed to support the tube.

There were no wires!

Don picked up the slender, glowing cylinder and held it between trembling fingers. Although it was delivering as much light as a two or three hundred watt bulb, it was cool to the touch. He examined it minutely. There was no possibility of concealed batteries.

The thumping of his heart was caused not by the fact that he had never seen a similar tube before, but because he had. He had never held one in his hands, though. The ones which his company had produced as experimental models had been unsuccessful at converting all of the radioactivity into light, and had, of necessity, been heavily shielded.

Right now, two of his colleagues back in the laboratory would still be searching for the right combination of fluorescent material and radioactive salts with which to make the simple, efficient, self-contained lighting unit that he was holding in his hand at this moment!

But this is impossible! he thought. *We're the only company that's working on this, and it's secret. There can't be any in actual production!*

And even if one had actually been successfully produced, how would it have fallen into the possession of POSAT, an Ancient Secret Society, The Perpetual Order of Seekers After Truth?

The conviction grew in Don's mind that here was something much deeper and more sinister than he would be able to cope with. He should have asked for help, should have stated his suspicions to the police or the FBI. Even now—

With sudden decision, he thrust the lighting tube into his pocket and stepped swiftly to the outer door. He grasped the knob and shook it impatiently when it stuck and refused to turn. He yanked at it. His impatience changed to panic. It was locked!

A soft sound behind him made him whirl about. The secretary had entered again through the inner door. She glanced at the vacant light bracket, then significantly at his bulging pocket. Her gaze was still as bland and innocent as when he had entered, but to Don she no longer seemed ordinary. Her very calmness in the face of his odd actions was distressingly ominous.

"Our Grand Chairman will see you now," she said in a quiet voice.

Don realized that he was half crouched in the position of an animal expecting attack. He straightened up with what dignity he could manage to find.

She opened the inner door again and Don followed her into what he supposed to be the office of the Grand Chairman of POSAT.

Instead he found himself on a balcony along the side of a vast room, which must have been the interior of the warehouse that he had noted outside. The girl motioned him toward the far end of the balcony, where a frosted glass door marked the office of the Grand Chairman.

• • •

Vocabulary words:
Find these words in the section, write the sentence they are used in, and write your own definition. If you are stuck, look it up in the dictionary, but still write a definition in your own words.

scrutiny
ominous
Comprehension/extension questions:

Why does the receptionist's reaction seem ominous to Alford?

What has he learned by the existence of the self-contained lightbulb? What conclusion would you come to?

• • •

But Don could not will his legs to move. His heart beat at the sight of the room below him. It was a laboratory, but a laboratory the like of which he had never seen before. Most of the equipment was unfamiliar to him. Whatever he did recognize was of a different design than he had ever used, and there was something about it that convinced him that this was more advanced. The men who bent busily over their instruments did not raise their eyes to the figures on the balcony.

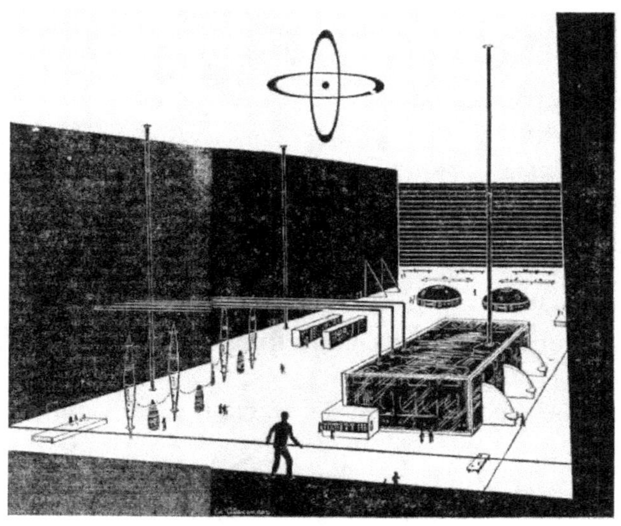

"Good Lord!" Don gasped. "That's an atomic reactor down there!" There could be no doubt about it, even though he could see it only obscurely through the bluish-green plastic shielding it.

His thoughts were so clamorous that he hardly realized that he had spoken aloud, or that the door at the end of the balcony had opened.

He was only dimly aware of the approaching footsteps as he speculated wildly on the nature of the shielding material. What could be so dense that only an inch would provide adequate shielding and yet remain semitransparent?

His scientist's mind applauded the genius who had developed it, even as the alarming conviction grew that he wouldn't—couldn't—be allowed to leave here anymore. Surely no man would be allowed to leave this place alive to tell the fantastic story to the world!

"Hello, Don," said a quiet voice beside him. "It's good to see you again."

"Dr. Crandon!" he heard his own voice reply. "*You're* the Grand Chairman of POSAT?"

He felt betrayed and sick at heart. The very voice with which Crandon had spoken conjured up visions of quiet lecture halls and his own youthful excitement at the masterful and orderly disclosure of scientific facts. To find him here in this mad and treacherous place— didn't anything make sense any longer?

"I think we have rather abused you, Don," Dr. Crandon continued. His voice sounded so gentle that Don found it hard to think there was any evil in it. "I can see that you are suspicious of us, and—yes— afraid."

• • •

Vocabulary words:
Find these words in the section, write the sentence they are used in, and write your own definition. If you are stuck, look it up in the dictionary, but still write a definition in your own words.

clamorous
conviction

Comprehension/extension questions:

What is Alford afraid of?

• • •

Don stared at the scene below him. After his initial glance to confirm his identification of Crandon, Don could not bear to look at him.

Crandon's voice suddenly hardened, became abrupt. "You're partly right about us, of course. I hate to think how many laws this organization has broken. Don't condemn us yet, though. You'll be a member yourself before the day is over."

Don was shocked by such confidence in his corruptibility.

"What do you use?" he asked bitterly. "Drugs? Hypnosis?"

Crandon sighed. "I forgot how little you know, Don. I have a long story to tell you. You'll find it hard to believe at first. But try to trust me. Try to believe me, as you once did. When I say that much of what POSAT does is illegal, I do not mean immoral. We're probably the most moral organization in the world. Get over the idea that you have stumbled into a den of thieves."

Crandon paused as though searching for words with which to continue.

"Did you notice the paintings in the waiting room as you entered?"

Don nodded, too bewildered to speak.

"They were donated by the founder of our Organization. They were part of his personal collection—which, incidentally, he bought from the artists themselves. He also designed the atomic reactor we use for power here in the laboratory."

"Then the pictures are modern," said Don, aware that his mouth was hanging open foolishly. "I thought one was a Titian—"

"It is," said Crandon. "We have several original Titians, although I really don't know too much about them."

"But how could a man alive *today* buy paintings from an artist of the Renaissance?"

"He is not alive today. POSAT is actually what our advertisements claim—an *ancient* secret society. Our founder has been dead for over four centuries."

"But you said that he designed your atomic reactor."

"Yes. This particular one has been in use for only twenty years, however."

Don's confusion was complete. Crandon looked at him kindly. "Let's start at the beginning," he said, and Don was back again in the classroom with the deep voice of Professor Crandon unfolding the pages of knowledge in clear and logical manner. "Four hundred years ago, in the time of the Italian Renaissance, a man lived who was a super-genius. His was the kind of incredible mentality that appears not in every generation, or even every century, but once in thousands of years.

"Probably the man who invented what we call the phonetic alphabet was one like him. That man lived seven thousand years ago in Mesopotamia, and his discovery was so original, so far from the natural course of man's thinking, that not once in the intervening seven thousand years has that device been rediscovered. It still exists only in the civilizations to which it has been passed on directly.

"The super-genius who was our founder was not a semanticist. He was a physical scientist and mathematician. Starting with the meager heritage that existed in these fields in his time, he began tackling physical puzzles one by one. Sitting in his study, using as his principal tool his own great mind, he invented calculus, developed the quantum theory of light, moved on to electromagnetic radiation and what we call Maxwell's equations—although, of course, he antedated Maxwell by centuries—developed the special and general theories of relativity, the tool of wave mechanics, and finally, toward the end of his life, he mathematically derived the packing fraction that describes the binding energy of nuclei—"

"But it can't be done," Don objected. "It's an observed phenomenon. It hasn't been derived." Every conservative instinct that he possessed cried out against this impossible fantasy. And yet—there sat the reactor, sheathed in its strange shield. Crandon watched the direction of Don's glance.

"Yes, the reactor," said Crandon. "He built one like it. It confirmed his theories. His calculations showed him something else too. He saw the destructive potentialities of an atomic explosion. He himself could not have built an atomic bomb; he didn't have the facilities. But his knowledge would have enabled other men to do so. He looked about him. He saw a political setup of warring principalities, rival states, intrigue, and squabbles over political power. Giving the men of his time atomic energy would have been like handing a baby a firecracker with a lighted fuse.

"What should he have done? Let his secrets die with him? He didn't think so. No one else in his age could have *derived* the knowledge that he did. But it was an age of brilliant men. Leonardo. Michelangelo. There were men capable of *learning* his science, even as men can learn it today. He gathered some of them together and founded this society. It served two purposes. It perpetuated his discoveries and at the same time it maintained the greatest secrecy about them. He urged that the secrets be kept until the time when men could use them safely. The other purpose was to make that time come about as soon as possible."

Crandon looked at Don's unbelieving face. "How can I make you see that it is the truth? Think of the eons that man or manlike creatures have walked the Earth. Think what a small fraction of that time is four hundred years. Is it so strange that atomic energy was discovered a little early, by this displacement in time that is so tiny after all?"

"But by one man," Don argued.

Crandon shrugged. "Compared with him, Don, you and I are stupid men. So are the scientists who slowly plodded down the same road he had come, stumbling first on one truth and then the succeeding one. We know that inventions and discoveries do not occur at random. Each is based on the one that preceded it. We are all aware of the phenomenon of simultaneous invention. The path to truth is a straight one. It is only our own stupidity that makes it seem slow and tortuous.

"He merely followed the straight path," Crandon finished simply.

• • •

Vocabulary words:
Find these words in the section, write the sentence they are used in, and write your own definition. If you are stuck, look it up in the dictionary, but still write a definition in your own words.

antedated
tortuous
Comprehension/extension questions:

Who do you think the founder was?

Is it conceivable that nuclear power could have been discovered that early?

• • •

Don's incredulity thawed a little. It was not entirely beyond the realm of possibility.

But if it were true! A vast panorama of possible achievements spread before him.

"Four hundred years!" he murmured with awe. "You've had four hundred years head-start on the rest of the world! What wonders you must have uncovered in that time!"

"Our technical achievements may disappoint you," warned Crandon. "Oh, they're way beyond anything that you are familiar with. You've undoubtedly noticed the shielding material on the reactor. That's a fairly recent development of our metallurgical department. There are other things in the laboratory that I can't even explain to you until you have caught up on the technical basis for understanding them.

"Our emphasis has not been on physical sciences, however, except as they contribute to our central project. We want to change civilization so that it can use physical science without disaster."

For a moment Don had been fired with enthusiasm. But at these words his heart sank.

"Then you've failed," he said bitterly. "In spite of centuries of advance warning, you've failed to change the rest of us enough to prevent us from trying to blow ourselves off the Earth. Here we are, still snarling and snapping at our neighbors' throats—and we've caught up with you. We have the atomic bomb. What's POSAT been doing all that time? Or have you found that human nature really can't be changed?"

"Come with me," said Crandon.

He led the way along the narrow balcony to another door, then down a steep flight of stairs. He opened a door at the bottom, and Don saw what must have been the world's largest computing machine.

"This is our answer," said Crandon. "Oh, rather, it's the tool by which we find our answer. For two centuries we have been working on the newest of the sciences— that of human motivation. Soon we will be ready to put some of our new knowledge to work. But you are right in one respect, we are working now against time. We must hurry if we are to save our civilization. That's why you are here. We have work for you to do. Will you join us, Don?"

"But why the hocus-pocus?" asked Don. "Why do you hide behind such a weird front as POSAT? Why do you advertise in magazines and invite just anyone to join? Why didn't you approach me directly, if you have work for me to do? And if you really have the answers to our problems, why haven't you gathered together all the scientists in the world to work on this project—before it's too late?"

Crandon took a sighing breath. "How I wish that we could do just that! But you forget that one of the prime purposes of our organization is to maintain the secrecy of our discoveries until they can be safely disclosed. We must be absolutely certain that anyone who enters this building will have joined POSAT before he leaves. What if we approached the wrong scientist? Centuries of accomplishment might be wasted if they attempted either to reveal it or to exploit it!

"Do you recall the questionnaires that you answered before you were invited here? We fed the answers to this machine and, as a result, we know more about how you will react in any given situation than you do yourself. Even if you should fail to join us, our secrets would be safe with you. Of course, we miss a few of the scientists who might be perfect material for our organization. You'd be surprised, though, at how clever our advertisements are at attracting exactly the men we want. With the help of our new science, we have baited our ads well, and we know how to maintain interest. Curiosity is, to the men we want, a powerful motivator."

"But what about the others?" asked Don. "There must be hundreds of applicants who would be of no use to you at all."

"Oh, yes," replied Crandon. "There are the mild religious fanatics. We enroll them as members and keep them interested by sending pamphlets in line with their interests. We even let them contribute to our upkeep, if they seem to want to. They never get beyond the reception room if they come to call on us. But they are additional people through whom we can act when the time finally comes.

"There are also the desperate people who try POSAT as a last resort—lost ones who can't find their direction in life. For them we put into practice some of our newly won knowledge. We rehabilitate them— anonymously, of course. Even find jobs or patch up homes. It's good practice for us.

"I think I've answered most of your questions, Don. But you haven't answered mine. Will you join us?"

Don looked solemnly at the orderly array of the computer before him. He had one more question.

"Will it really work? Can it actually tell you how to motivate the stubborn, quarrelsome, opinionated people one finds on this Earth?"

Crandon smiled. "You're here, aren't you?"

Don nodded, his tense features relaxing.

"Enroll me as a member," he said.

WHAT IS POSAT?

• • •

Vocabulary words:
Find these words in the section, write the sentence they are used in, and write your own definition. If you are stuck, look it up in the dictionary, but still write a definition in your own words.

metallurgical
exploit
Comprehension/extension questions:

Why does POSAT exist?

Why would Alford join them?

What is POSAT, by Phyllis Sterling Smith, Published September 1951

Phyllis Sterling Smith published a handful of short stories in 1951-1952 and currently resides in Washington.

THE MAN OUTSIDE

By EVELYN E. SMITH
Illustrated by DILLON

*No one, least of all Martin, could dispute
that a man's life should be guarded by his
kin—but by those who hadn't been born yet?*

Nobody in the neighborhood was surprised when Martin's mother disappeared and Ninian came to take care of him. Mothers had a way of disappearing around those parts and the kids were often better off without them. Martin was no exception. He'd never had it this good while he was living with his old lady. As for his father, Martin had never had one. He'd been a war baby, born of one of the tides of soldiers—enemies and allies, both—that had engulfed the country in successive waves and bought or taken the women. So there was no trouble that way.

Sometimes he wondered who Ninian really was. Obviously that story about her coming from the future was just a gag. Besides, if she really was his great-great-grand-daughter, as she said, why would she tell him to call her "*Aunt Ninian*"? Maybe he was only eleven, but he'd been around and he knew just what the score was. At first he'd thought maybe she was some new kind of social worker, but she acted a little too crazy for that.

He loved to bait her, as he had loved to bait his mother. It was safer with Ninian, though, because when he pushed her too far, she would cry instead of mopping up the floor with him.

"But I can't understand," he would say, keeping his face straight. "Why do you have to come from the future to protect me against your cousin Conrad?"

"Because he's coming to kill you."

"Why should he kill me? I ain't done him nothing."

Ninian sighed. "He's dissatisfied with the current social order and killing you is part of an elaborate plan he's formulated to change it. You wouldn't understand."

"You're damn right. I *don't* understand. What's it all about in straight gas?"

"Oh, just don't ask any questions," Ninian said petulantly. "When you get older, someone will explain the whole thing to you."

So Martin held his peace, because, on the whole, he liked things the way they were. Ninian really was the limit, though. All the people he knew lived in scabrous tenement apartments like his, but she seemed to think it was disgusting.

"So if you don't like it, clean it up," he suggested.

She looked at him as if he were out of his mind.

"Hire a maid, then!" he jeered.

And darned if that dope didn't go out and get a woman to come clean up the place! He was so embarrassed, he didn't even dare show his face in the streets—especially with the women buttonholing him and demanding to know what gave. They tried talking to Ninian, but she certainly knew how to give them the cold shoulder.

One day the truant officer came to ask why Martin hadn't been coming to school. Very few of the neighborhood kids attended classes very regularly, so this was just routine. But Ninian didn't know that and she went into a real tizzy, babbling that Martin had been sick and would make up the work. Martin nearly did get sick from laughing so hard inside.

But he laughed out of the other side of his mouth when she went out and hired a private tutor for him. A tutor—in that neighborhood! Martin had to beat up every kid on the block before he could walk a step without hearing "Fancy Pants!" yelled after him.

Ninian worried all the time. It wasn't that she cared what these people thought of her, for she made no secret of regarding them as little better than animals, but she was shy of attracting attention. There were an awful lot of people in that neighborhood who felt exactly the same way, only she didn't know that, either. She was really pretty dumb, Martin thought, for all her fancy lingo.

"It's so hard to think these things out without any prior practical application to go by," she told him.

He nodded, knowing what she meant was that everything was coming out wrong. But he didn't try to help her; he just watched to see what she'd do next. Already he had begun to assume the detached role of a spectator.

When it became clear that his mother was never going to show up again, Ninian bought one of those smallish, almost identical houses that mushroom on the fringes of a city after every war, particularly where intensive bombing has created a number of desirable building sites.

"This is a much better neighborhood for a boy to grow up in," she declared. "Besides, it's easier to keep an eye on you here."

And keep an eye on him she did—she or a rather foppish young man who came to stay with them occasionally. Martin was told to call him Uncle Raymond.

From time to time, there were other visitors— Uncles Ives and Bartholomew and Olaf, Aunts Ottillie and Grania and Lalage, and many more—all cousins to one another, he was told, all descendants of his.

• • •

Vocabulary words:
Find these words in the section, write the sentence they are used in, and write your own definition. If you are stuck, look it up in the dictionary, but still write a definition in your own words.

successive
scabrous

Comprehension/extension questions:

What does Martin think of Ninian?

Why doesn't he believe her story?

• • •

Martin was never left alone for a minute. He wasn't allowed to play with the other kids in the new neighborhood. Not that their parents would have let them, anyway. The adults obviously figured that if a one-car family hired private tutors for their kid, there must be something pretty wrong with him. So Martin and Ninian were just as conspicuous as before. But he didn't tip her off. She was grown up; she was supposed to know better than he did.

He lived well. He had food to eat that he'd never dreamed of before, warm clothes that no one had ever worn before him. He was surrounded by more luxury than he knew what to do with.

The furniture was the latest New Grand Rapids African modern. There were tidy, colorful Picasso and Braque prints on the walls. And every inch of the floor was modestly covered by carpeting, though the walls were mostly unabashed glass. There were hot water and heat all the time and a freezer well stocked with food— somewhat erratically chosen, for Ninian didn't know much about meals.

The non-glass part of the house was of neat, natural-toned wood, with a neat green lawn in front and a neat parti-colored garden in back.

Martin missed the old neighborhood, though. He missed having other kids to play with. He even missed his mother. Sure, she hadn't given him enough to eat and she'd beaten him up so hard sometimes that she'd nearly killed him—but then there had also been times when she'd hugged and kissed him and soaked his collar with her tears. She'd done all she could for him, supporting him in the only way she knew how—and if respectable society didn't like it, the hell with respectable society.

From Ninian and her cousins, there was only an impersonal kindness. They made no bones about the fact that they were there only to carry out a rather unpleasant duty. Though they were in the house with him, in their minds and in their talk they were living in another world—a world of warmth and peace and plenty where nobody worked, except in the government service or the essential professions. And they seemed to think even that kind of job was pretty low-class, though better than actually doing anything with the hands.

In their world, Martin came to understand, nobody worked with hands; everything was done by machinery. All the people ever did was wear pretty clothes and have good times and eat all they wanted. There was no devastation, no war, no unhappiness, none of the concomitants of normal living.

It was then that Martin began to realize that either the whole lot of them were insane, or what Ninian had told him at first was the truth. They came from the future.

• • •

Vocabulary words:
Find these words in the section, write the sentence they are used in, and write your own definition. If you are stuck, look it up in the dictionary, but still write a definition in your own words.

conspicuous
erratically
concomitants
Comprehension/extension questions:

What does Martin like about the new relatives?

What does he miss about his mother?

• • •

When Martin was sixteen, Raymond took him aside for the talk Ninian had promised five years before.

"The whole thing's all my brother Conrad's fault. You see, he's an idealist," Raymond explained, pronouncing the last word with distaste.

Martin nodded gravely. He was a quiet boy now, his brief past a dim and rather ridiculous memory. Who could ever imagine him robbing a grocery store or wielding a broken bottle now? He still was rather undersized and he'd read so much that he'd weakened his eyes and had to wear glasses. His face was pallid, because he spent little time in the sun, and his speech rather overbred, his mentors from the future having carefully eradicated all current vulgarities.

"And Conrad really got upset over the way Earth has been exploiting the not so intelligent life-forms on the other planets," Raymond continued. "Which *is* distressing—though, of course, it's not as if they were people. Besides, the government has been talking about passing laws to do away with the—well, abuses and things like that, and I'm sure someday everything will come out all right. However, Conrad is so impatient."

"I thought, in your world, machines did all the work," Martin suggested.

"I've told you—our world is precisely the same as this one!" Raymond snapped. "We just come a couple of centuries or so later, that's all. But remember, our interests are identical. We're virtually the same people... although it is amazing what a difference two hundred odd years of progress and polish can make in a species, isn't it?"

He continued more mildly: "However, even you ought to be able to understand that we can't make machinery without metal. We need food. All that sort of thing comes from the out-system planets. And, on those worlds, it's far cheaper to use native labor than to ship out all that expensive machinery. After all, if we didn't give the natives jobs, how would they manage to live?"

"How did they live before? Come to think of it, if you don't work, how do *you* live now?... I don't mean in the now for me, but the now for you," Martin explained laboriously. It was so difficult to live in the past and think in the future.

"I'm trying to talk to you as if you were an adult," Raymond said, "but if you will persist in these childish interruptions—"

"I'm sorry," Martin said.

But he wasn't, for by now he had little respect left for any of his descendants. They were all exceedingly handsome and cultivated young people, with superior educations, smooth ways of speaking and considerable self-confidence, but they just weren't very bright. And he had discovered that Raymond was perhaps the most intelligent of the lot. Somewhere in that relatively short span of time, his line or—more frightening—his race had lost something vital.

Unaware of the near-contempt in which his young ancestor held him, Raymond went on blandly: "Anyhow, Conrad took it upon himself to feel particularly guilty, because, he decided, if it hadn't been for the fact that our great-grandfather discovered the super-drive, we might never have reached the stars. Which is ridiculous—his feeling guilty, I mean. Perhaps a great-grandfather is responsible for his great-grandchildren, but a great-grandchild can hardly be held accountable for his great-grandfather."

"How about a great-great-grandchild?" Martin couldn't help asking.

Raymond flushed a delicate pink. "Do you want to hear the rest of this or don't you?"

"Oh, I do!" Martin said. He had pieced the whole thing together for himself long since, but he wanted to hear how Raymond would put it.

"Unfortunately, Professor Farkas has just perfected the time transmitter. Those government scientists are so infernally officious—always inventing such senseless things. It's supposed to be hush-hush, but you know how news will leak out when one is always desperate for a fresh topic of conversation."

Anyhow, Raymond went on to explain, Conrad had bribed one of Farkas' assistants for a set of the plans. Conrad's idea had been to go back in time and "eliminate!" their common great-grandfather. In that way, there would be no space-drive, and, hence, the Terrestrials would never get to the other planets and oppress the local aborigines.

"Sounds like a good way of dealing with the problem," Martin observed.

Raymond looked annoyed. "It's the *adolescent* way," he said, "to do away with it, rather than find a solution. Would you destroy a whole society in order to root out a single injustice?"

"Not if it were a good one otherwise."

"Well, there's your answer. Conrad got the apparatus built, or perhaps he built it himself. One doesn't inquire too closely into such matters. But when it came to the point, Conrad couldn't bear the idea of eliminating our great-grandfather—because our great-grandfather was such a *good* man, you know." Raymond's expressive upper lip curled. "So Conrad decided to go further back still and get rid of his great-grandfather's father—who'd been, by all accounts, a pretty worthless character."

"That would be me, I suppose," Martin said quietly.

Raymond turned a deep rose. "Well, doesn't that just go to prove you mustn't believe everything you hear?" The next sentence tumbled out in a rush. "I wormed the whole thing out of him and all of us—the other cousins and me—held a council of war, as it were, and we decided it was our moral duty to go back in time ourselves and protect you." He beamed at Martin.

The boy smiled slowly. "Of course. You had to. If Conrad succeeded in *eliminating* me, then none of you would exist, would you?"

Raymond frowned. Then he shrugged cheerfully. "Well, you didn't really suppose we were going to all this trouble and expense out of sheer altruism, did you?" he asked, turning on the charm which all the cousins possessed to a consternating degree.

Martin had, of course, no illusions on that score; he had learned long ago that nobody did anything for nothing. But saying so was unwise.

"We bribed another set of plans out of another of the professor's assistants," Raymond continued, as if Martin had answered, "and—ah—induced a handicraft enthusiast to build the gadget for us."

Induced, Martin knew, could have meant anything from blackmail to the use of the iron maiden.[2]

---

[2] A medieval torture device.

"Then we were all ready to forestall Conrad. If one of us guarded you night and day, he would never be able to carry out his plot. So we made our counter-plan, set the machine as far back as it would go—and here we are!"

"I see," Martin said.

Raymond didn't seem to think he really did. "After all," he pointed out defensively, "whatever our motives, it has turned into a good thing for you. Nice home, cultured companions, all the contemporary conveniences, plus some handy anachronisms—I don't see what more you could ask for. You're getting the best of all possible worlds. Of course Ninian *was* a ninny to locate in a mercantile suburb where any little thing out of the way will cause talk. How thankful I am that our era has completely disposed of the mercantiles—"

"What did you do with them?" Martin asked.

But Raymond rushed on: "Soon as Ninian goes and I'm in full charge, we'll get a more isolated place and run it on a far grander scale. Ostentation—that's the way to live here and now; the richer you are, the more eccentricity you can get away with. And," he added, "I might as well be as comfortable as possible while I suffer through this wretched historical stint."

"So Ninian's going," said Martin, wondering why the news made him feel curiously desolate. Because, although he supposed he liked her in a remote kind of way, he had no fondness for her—or she, he knew, for him.

"Well, five years is rather a long stretch for any girl to spend in exile," Raymond explained, "even though our life spans are a bit longer than yours. Besides, you're getting too old now to be under petticoat government." He looked inquisitively at Martin. "You're not going to go all weepy and make a scene when she leaves, are you?"

"No...." Martin said hesitantly. "Oh, I suppose I will miss her. But we aren't very close, so it won't make a real difference." That was the sad part: he already knew it wouldn't make a difference.

Raymond clapped him on the shoulder. "I knew you weren't a sloppy sentimentalist like Conrad. Though you do have rather a look of him, you know."

Suddenly that seemed to make Conrad real. Martin felt a vague stirring of alarm. He kept his voice composed, however. "How do you plan to protect me when he comes?"

"Well, each one of us is armed to the teeth, of course," Raymond said with modest pride, displaying something that looked like a child's combination spaceman's gun and death ray, but which, Martin had no doubt, was a perfectly genuine—and lethal— weapon. "And we've got a rather elaborate burglar alarm system."

Martin inspected the system and made one or two changes in the wiring which, he felt, would increase its efficiency. But still he was dubious. "Maybe it'll work on someone coming from outside this *house*, but do you think it will work on someone coming from outside this *time*?"

"Never fear—it has a temporal radius," Raymond replied. "Factory guarantee and all that."

"Just to be on the safe side," Martin said, "I think I'd better have one of those guns, too."

"A splendid idea!" enthused Raymond. "I was just about to think of that myself!"

• • •

Vocabulary words:
Find these words in the section, write the sentence they are used in, and write your own definition. If you are stuck, look it up in the dictionary, but still write a definition in your own words.

vulgarities
officious
altruism
anachronisms
Comprehension/extension questions:

What kind of society do Martin's descendants live in?

Would you want to live in their world?

• • •

When it came time for the parting, it was Ninian who cried—tears at her own inadequacy, Martin knew, not of sorrow. He was getting skillful at understanding his descendants, far better than they at understanding him. But then they never really tried. Ninian kissed him wetly on the cheek and said she was sure everything would work out all right and that she'd come see him again. She never did, though, except at the very last.

Raymond and Martin moved into a luxurious mansion in a remote area. The site proved a well-chosen one; when the Second Atomic War came, half a dozen years later, they weren't touched. Martin was never sure whether this had been sheer luck or expert planning. Probably luck, because his descendants were exceedingly inept planners.

Few people in the world then could afford to live as stylishly as Martin and his guardian. The place not only contained every possible convenience and gadget but was crammed with bibelots[3] and antiques, carefully chosen by Raymond and disputed by Martin, for, to the man from the future, all available artifacts were antiques. Otherwise, Martin accepted his new surroundings. His sense of wonder had become dulled by now and the pink pseudo-Spanish castle— "architecturally dreadful, of course," Raymond had said, "but so hilariously typical" —impressed him far less than had the suburban split-level aquarium.

"How about a moat?" Martin suggested when they first came. "It seems to go with a castle."

"Do you think a moat could stop Conrad?" Raymond asked, amused.

"No," Martin smiled, feeling rather silly, "but it would make the place seem safer somehow."

---

[3] trinkets

The threat of Conrad was beginning to make him grow more and more nervous. He got Raymond's permission to take two suits of armor that stood in the front hall and present them to a local museum, because several times he fancied he saw them move. He also became an adept with the ray gun and changed the surrounding landscape quite a bit with it, until Raymond warned that this might lead Conrad to them.

During those early years, Martin's tutors were exchanged for the higher-degreed ones that were now needful. The question inevitably arose of what the youth's vocation in that life was going to be. At least twenty of the cousins came back through time to hold one of their vigorous family councils. Martin was still young enough to enjoy such occasions, finding them vastly superior to all other forms of entertainment.

"This sort of problem wouldn't arise in our day, Martin," Raymond commented as he took his place at the head of the table, "because, unless one specifically feels a call to some profession or other, one just—well, drifts along happily."

"Ours is a wonderful world," Grania sighed at Martin. "I only wish we could take you there. I'm sure you would like it."

"Don't be a fool, Grania!" Raymond snapped. "Well, Martin, have you made up your mind what you want to be?"

Martin affected to think. "A physicist," he said, not without malice. "Or perhaps an engineer."

There was a loud, excited chorus of dissent. He chuckled inwardly.

"Can't do that," Ives said. "Might pick up some concepts from us. Don't know how; none of us knows a thing about science. But it could happen. Subconscious osmosis, if there is such a thing. That way, you might invent something ahead of time. And the fellow we got the plans from particularly cautioned us against that. Changing history. Dangerous."

"Might mess up our time frightfully," Bartholomew contributed, "though, to be perfectly frank, I can't quite understand how."

"I am not going to sit down and explain the whole thing to you all over again, Bart!" Raymond said impatiently. "Well, Martin?"

"What would you suggest?" Martin asked.

"How about becoming a painter? Art is eternal. And quite gentlemanly. Besides, artists are always expected to be either behind or ahead of their times."

"Furthermore," Ottillie added, "one more artist couldn't make much difference in history. There were so many of them all through the ages."

Martin couldn't hold back his question. "What was I, actually, in that other time?"

There was a chilly silence.

"Let's not talk about it, dear," Lalage finally said. "Let's just be thankful we've saved you from *that*!"

So drawing teachers were engaged and Martin became a very competent second-rate artist. He knew he would never be able to achieve first rank because, even though he was still so young, his work was almost purely intellectual. The only emotion he seemed able to feel was fear—the ever-present fear that someday he would turn a corridor and walk into a man who looked like him—a man who wanted to kill him for the sake of an ideal.

But the fear did not show in Martin's pictures. They were pretty pictures.

• • •

Vocabulary words:
Find these words in the section, write the sentence they are used in, and write your own definition. If you are stuck, look it up in the dictionary, but still write a definition in your own words.

inept
osmosis
Comprehension/extension questions:

What was Martin in the previous iteration?

Why don't the relatives want him to follow his former career path?

• • •

Cousin Ives—now that Martin was older, he was told to call the descendants *cousin*—next assumed guardianship. Ives took his responsibilities more seriously than the others did. He even arranged to have Martin's work shown at an art gallery. The paintings received critical approval, but failed to evoke any enthusiasm. The modest sale they enjoyed was mostly to interior decorators. Museums were not interested.

"Takes time," Ives tried to reassure him. "One day they'll be buying your pictures, Martin. Wait and see."

Ives was the only one of the descendants who seemed to think of Martin as an individual. When his efforts to make contact with the other young man failed, he got worried and decided that what Martin needed was a change of air and scenery.

"'Course you can't go on the Grand Tour. Your son hasn't invented space travel yet. But we can go see this world. What's left of it. Tourists always like ruins best, anyway."

So he drew on the family's vast future resources and bought a yacht, which Martin christened *The Interregnum*. They traveled about from sea to ocean and from ocean to sea, touching at various ports and making trips inland. Martin saw the civilized world—mostly in fragments; the nearly intact semi-civilized world and the uncivilized world, much the same as it had been for centuries. It was like visiting an enormous museum; he couldn't seem to identify with his own time any more.

The other cousins appeared to find the yacht a congenial headquarters, largely because they could spend so much time far away from the contemporary inhabitants of the planet and relax and be themselves. So they never moved back to land. Martin spent the rest of his life on *The Interregnum*. He felt curiously safer from Conrad there, although there was no valid reason why an ocean should stop a traveler through time.

More cousins were in residence at once than ever before, because they came for the ocean voyage. They spent most of their time aboard ship, giving each other parties and playing an *avant-garde* form of shuffleboard and gambling on future sporting events. That last usually ended in a brawl, because one cousin was sure to accuse another of having got advance information about the results.

Martin didn't care much for their company and associated with them only when not to have done so would have been palpably rude. And, though they were gregarious young people for the most part, they didn't court his society. He suspected that he made them feel uncomfortable.

He rather liked Ives, though. Sometimes the two of them would be alone together; then Ives would tell Martin of the future world he had come from. The picture drawn by Raymond and Ninian had not been entirely accurate, Ives admitted. True, there was no war or poverty on Earth proper, but that was because there were only a couple of million people left on the planet. It was an enclave for the highly privileged, highly interbred aristocracy, to which Martin's descendants belonged by virtue of their distinguished ancestry.

"Rather feudal, isn't it?" Martin asked.

Ives agreed, adding that the system had, however, been deliberately planned, rather than the result of haphazard natural development. Everything potentially unpleasant, like the mercantiles, had been deported.

"Not only natives livin' on the other worlds," Ives said as the two of them stood at the ship's rail, surrounded by the limitless expanse of some ocean or other. "People, too. Mostly lower classes, except for officials and things. With wars and want and suffering," he added regretfully, "same as in your day.... Like now, I mean," he corrected himself. "Maybe it *is* worse, the way Conrad thinks. More planets for us to make trouble on. Three that were habitable aren't anymore. Bombed. Very thorough job."

"Oh," Martin murmured, trying to sound shocked, horrified—interested, even.

"Sometimes I'm not altogether sure Conrad was wrong," Ives said, after a pause. "Tried to keep us from getting to the stars, hurting the people—I expect you could call them people—there. Still—" he smiled shamefacedly— "couldn't stand by and see my own way of life destroyed, could I?"

"I suppose not," Martin said.

"Would take moral courage. I don't have it. None of us does, except Conrad, and even he—" Ives looked out over the sea. "Must be a better way out than Conrad's," he said without conviction. "And everything will work out all right in the end. Bound to. No sense to—to anything, if it doesn't." He glanced wistfully at Martin.

"I hope so," said Martin. But he couldn't hope; he couldn't feel; he couldn't even seem to care.

During all this time, Conrad still did not put in an appearance. Martin had gotten to be such a crack shot with the ray pistol that he almost wished his descendant would show up, so there would be some excitement. But he didn't come. And Martin got to thinking....

He always felt that if any of the cousins could have come to realize the basic flaw in the elaborate plan they had concocted, it would have been Ives. However, when the yacht touched at Tierra del Fuego one bitter winter, Ives took a severe chill. They sent for a doctor from the future—one of the descendants who had been eccentric enough to take a medical degree—but he wasn't able to save Ives. The body was buried in the frozen ground at Ushuaia, on the southern tip of the continent, a hundred years or more before the date of his birth.

A great many of the cousins turned up at the simple ceremony. All were dressed in overwhelming black and showed a great deal of grief. Raymond read the burial service, because they didn't dare summon a clerical cousin from the future; they were afraid he might prove rather stuffy about the entire undertaking.

"He died for all of us," Raymond concluded his funeral eulogy over Ives, "so his death was not in vain."

But Martin disagreed.

• • •

Vocabulary words:
Find these words in the section, write the sentence they are used in, and write your own definition. If you are stuck, look it up in the dictionary, but still write a definition in your own words.

gregarious
distinguished

Comprehension/extension questions:

Why would Martin call the yacht the Interregnum? What did that mean to him?

• • •

The ceaseless voyaging began again. *The Interregnum* voyaged to every ocean and every sea. Some were blue and some green and some dun. After a while, Martin couldn't tell one from another. Cousin after cousin came to watch over him and eventually they were as hard for him to tell apart as the different oceans.

All the cousins were young, for, though they came at different times in his life, they had all started out from the same time in theirs. Only the young ones had been included in the venture; they did not trust their elders.

As the years went by, Martin began to lose even his detached interest in the land and its doings. Although the yacht frequently touched port for fuel or supplies—it was more economical to purchase them in that era than to have them shipped from the future—he seldom went ashore, and then only at the urging of a newly assigned cousin anxious to see the sights. Most of the time Martin spent in watching the sea—and sometimes he painted it. There seemed to be a depth to his seascapes that his other work lacked.

When he was pressed by the current cousin to make a land visit somewhere, he decided to exhibit a few of his sea paintings. That way, he could fool himself into thinking that there was some purpose to this journey. He'd come to believe that perhaps what his life lacked was purpose, and for a while he kept looking for meaning everywhere, to the cousin's utter disgust.

"Eat, drink and be merry, or whatever you Romans say when you do as you do," the cousin—who was rather woolly in history; the descendants were scraping bottom now—advised.

Martin showed his work in Italy, so that the cousin could be disillusioned by the current crop of Romans. He found that neither purpose nor malice was enough; he was still immeasurably bored. However, a museum bought two of the paintings. Martin thought of Ives and felt an uncomfortable pang of a sensation he could no longer understand.

"Where do you suppose Conrad has been all this time?" Martin idly asked the current cousin—who was passing as his nephew by now.

The young man jumped, then glanced around him uncomfortably. "Conrad's a very shrewd fellow," he whispered. "He's biding his time—waiting until we're off guard. And then—pow!—he'll attack!"

"Oh, I see," Martin said.

He had often fancied that Conrad would prove to be the most stimulating member of the whole generation. But it seemed unlikely that he would ever have a chance for a conversation with the young man. More than one conversation, anyhow.

"When he does show up, I'll protect you," the cousin vowed, touching his ray gun. "You haven't a thing to worry about."

Martin smiled with all the charm he'd had nothing to do but acquire. "I have every confidence in you," he told his descendant. He himself had given up carrying a gun long ago.

There was a war in the Northern Hemisphere and so *The Interregnum* voyaged to southern waters. There was a war in the south and they hid out in the Arctic. All the nations became too drained of power—fuel and man and will—to fight, so there was a sterile peace for a long time. *The Interregnum* roamed the seas restlessly, with her load of passengers from the future, plus one bored and aging contemporary. She bore big guns now, because of the ever-present danger of pirates.

Perhaps it was the traditionally bracing effect of sea air—perhaps it was the sheltered life—but Martin lived to be a very old man. He was a hundred and four when his last illness came. It was a great relief when the family doctor, called in again from the future, said there was no hope. Martin didn't think he could have borne another year of life.

All the cousins gathered at the yacht to pay their last respects to their progenitor. He saw Ninian again, after all these years, and Raymond—all the others, dozens of them, thronging around his bed, spilling out of the cabin and into the passageways and out onto the deck, making their usual clamor, even though their voices were hushed.

Only Ives was missing. He'd been the lucky one, Martin knew. He had been spared the tragedy that was going to befall these blooming young people—all the same age as when Martin had last seen them and doomed never to grow any older. Underneath their masks of woe, he could see relief at the thought that at last they were going to be rid of their responsibility. And underneath Martin's death mask lay an impersonal pity for those poor, stupid descendants of his who had blundered so irretrievably.

There was only one face which Martin had never seen before. It wasn't a strange face, however, because Martin had seen one very like it in the looking glass when he was a young man.

"You must be Conrad," Martin called across the cabin in a voice that was still clear. "I've been looking forward to meeting you for some time."

The other cousins whirled to face the newcomer.

"You're too late, Con," Raymond gloated for the whole generation. "He's lived out his life."

"But he hasn't lived out his life," Conrad contradicted. "He's lived out the life *you* created for him. And for yourselves, too."

For the first time, Martin saw compassion in the eyes of one of his lineage and found it vaguely disturbing. It didn't seem to belong there.

"Don't you realize even yet," Conrad went on, "that as soon as he goes, you'll go, too—present, past, future, wherever you are, you'll go up in the air like puffs of smoke?"

"What do you mean?" Ninian quavered, her soft, pretty face alarmed.

Martin answered Conrad's rueful smile, but left the explanations up to him. It was his show, after all.

"Because you will never have existed," Conrad said. "You have no right to existence; it was you yourselves who watched him all the time, so he didn't have a chance to lead a normal life, get married, *have children....*"

Most of the cousins gasped as the truth began to percolate through.

"I knew from the very beginning," Conrad finished, "that I didn't have to do anything at all. I just had to wait and you would destroy yourselves."

"I don't understand," Bartholomew protested, searching the faces of the cousins closest to him. "What does he mean, we have never existed? We're here, aren't we? What—"

"Shut up!" Raymond snapped. He turned on Martin. "You don't seem surprised."

The old man grinned. "I'm not. I figured it all out years ago."

At first, he had wondered what he should do. Would it be better to throw them into a futile panic by telling them or to do nothing? He had decided on the latter; that was the role they had assigned him—to watch and wait and keep out of things—and that was the role he would play.

"You knew all the time and you didn't tell us!" Raymond spluttered. "After we'd been so good to you, making a gentleman out of you instead of a criminal.... That's right," he snarled, "a criminal! An alcoholic, a thief, a derelict! How do you like that?"

"Sounds like a rich, full life," Martin said wistfully.

What an exciting existence they must have done him out of! But then, he couldn't help thinking, he—he and Conrad together, of course—had done them out of *any* kind of existence. It wasn't his responsibility, though; he had done nothing but let matters take whatever course was destined for them. If only he could be sure that it was the better course, perhaps he wouldn't feel that nagging sense of guilt inside him. Strange—where, in his hermetic life, could he possibly have developed such a queer thing as a conscience?

"Then we've wasted all this time," Ninian sobbed, "all this energy, all this money, for nothing!"

"But you were nothing to begin with," Martin told them. And then, after a pause, he added, "I only wish I could be sure there had been some purpose to this."

He didn't know whether it was approaching death that dimmed his sight, or whether the frightened crowd that pressed around him was growing shadowy.

"I wish I could feel that some good had been done in letting you be wiped out of existence," he went on voicing his thoughts. "But I know that the same thing that happened to your worlds and my world will happen all over again. To other people, in other times, but again. It's bound to happen. There isn't any hope for humanity."

One man couldn't really change the course of human history, he told himself. Two men, that was— one real, one a shadow.

Conrad came close to the old man's bed. He was almost transparent.

"No," he said, "there is hope. They didn't know the time transmitter works two ways. I used it for going into the past only once—just this once. But I've gone into the future with it many times. And—" he pressed Martin's hand— "believe me, what I did—what *we* did, you and I—serves a purpose. It will change things for the better. Everything is going to be all right."

Was Conrad telling him the truth, Martin wondered, or was he just giving the conventional reassurance to the dying? More than that, was he trying to convince himself that what he had done was the right thing?

Every cousin had assured Martin that things were going to be all right.

Was Conrad *actually* different from the rest?

His plan had worked and the others' hadn't, but then all his plan had consisted of was doing nothing. That was all he and Martin had done… nothing. Were they absolved of all responsibility merely because they had stood aside and taken advantage of the others' weaknesses?

"Why," Martin said to himself, "in a sense, it could be said that I have fulfilled my original destiny—that I am a criminal."

Well, it didn't matter; whatever happened, no one could hold him to blame. He held no stake in the future that was to come. It was other men's future—other men's problem. He died very peacefully then, and, since he was the only one left on the ship, there was nobody to bury him.

The unmanned yacht drifted about the seas for years and gave rise to many legends, none of them as unbelievable as the truth.

• • •

Vocabulary words:
Find these words in the section, write the sentence they are used in, and write your own definition. If you are stuck, look it up in the dictionary, but still write a definition in your own words.

progenitor
percolate
hermetic

Comprehension/extension questions:

Did Martin make the right choice? Did Conrad?

What effect do you think their choices had on the distant future, which Conrad saw?

Look up 'the grandfather paradox.'

The Man Outside, by Evelyn E. Smith, Published August 1957

Evelyn E. Smith was born in New York City, New York July 25, 1922 and died July 4, 2000. She wrote many short stories in the 1950s to 19602 and authored four novels. She also wrote under the name Delphine C. Lyons.

SWENSON, DISPATCHER

By R. DeWITT MILLER
Illustrated by FRANCIS

*There were no vacuums in Space Regulations,
so Swenson—well, you might say he knew how to
plot courses through sub-ether legality!*

It was on October 15, 2177, that Swenson staggered into the offices of Acme Interplanetary Express and demanded a job as dispatcher.

They threw him out. They forgot to lock the door. The next time they threw him out, they remembered to lock the door but forgot the window.

The dingy office was on the ground floor and Swenson was a tall man. When he came in the window, the distraught Acme Board of Directors realized that they had something unusual in the way of determined drunks to deal with.

Acme was one of the small hermaphroditic companies—hauling mainly freight, but shipping a few passengers—which were an outgrowth of the most recent war to create peace.

During that violent conflict, America had established bases throughout the Solar System. These required an endless stream of items necessary for human existence.

While the hostilities lasted, the small outfits were vital and for that reason prospered. They hauled oxygen, food, spare parts, whisky, atomic slugs, professional women, uniforms, paper for quadruplicate reports, cigarettes, and all the other impedimenta of war-time life.

With the outbreak of peace, such companies faced a precarious, devil-take-the-hindmost type of existence.

The day that Swenson arrived had been grim even for Acme. Dovorkin, the regular dispatcher, had been fired that morning. He had succeeded in leaving the schedule in a nightmarish muddle.

And on Dovorkin's vacant desk lay the last straw—a Special Message.

Acme Interplanetary Express
147 Z Street
New York

Your atomic-converted ship Number 7 is hereby grounded at Luna City, Moon, until demurrage bill paid. Your previous violations of Space Regulations make our action mandatory.

Planetary Commerce Commission

SWENSON, DISPATCHER

The Acme Board of Directors was inured to accepting the inevitable. They had heard rumors along Blaster's Alley of Swenson's reputation, which ranged from brilliance, through competence, to insanity. So they shrugged and hired him.

His first act was to order a case of beer. His second was to look at what Dovorkin had left of a Dispatch Sheet.

• • •

Vocabulary words:
Find these words in the section, write the sentence they are used in, and write your own definition. If you are stuck, look it up in the dictionary, but still write a definition in your own words.

hermaphroditic
impedimenta
demurrage

Comprehension/extension questions:

What is the tone of this short story?

What do you like or dislike about it?

• • •

"Number 5 is still blasting through the astraloids. It should be free-falling. Why the hell isn't it?"

Old Mister Cerobie, Chairman of the Board, said quietly: "Before you begin your work, we would like a bit of information. What is your full name?"

"Patrick M. Swenson."

"What does the M stand for?"

"I don't know."

"Why not?"

"My mother never told me. I don't think she knows. In the name of God, why don't you send Number 3...."

"What's your nationality?"

"I'm supposed to be a Swede."

"What do you mean, 'supposed'?"

"Will you open one of those beers?"

"I asked you...."

Swenson made a notation on the Dispatch Sheet and spun around in the swivel chair. "I was born on a *Swallow Class* ship in space between the Moon and Earth. My mother said my father was a Swede. She was Irish. I was delivered and circumcised by a rabbi who happened to be on board. The ship was of Venutian registry, but was owned by a Czechoslovakian company. Now you figure it out."

"How did you happen to come here?"

"I met Dovorkin in a bar. He told me that you were in trouble. You are. Is one of the Moulton Trust's ships at Luna City?"

"Yes."

"Then that's why you're grounded. They've got an in with the Planetary Commerce Commission. What's the demurrage?"

"Seventy-six thousand dollars."

"Can you raise it?"

"No."

Swenson glanced at the sheet. "How come Number 2 is in New York?"

"We're waiting for additional cargo. We have half a load of snuff for Mars. And we've been promised half a load of canned goods for Luna City. It's reduced rate freight that another company can't handle."

"Dovorkin told me about the snuff. That's a starter, anyway." Swenson turned back to the Dispatch Sheet and muttered to himself: "Always a good thing to have snuff for Mars."

Mister Cerobie became strangely interested.

"Why?"

Swenson paid no attention. "What are you taking a split load for?"

"We had no choice."

"You know damn well that the broken-down old stovepipes you buy from war surplus are too slow to handle split loads. Who promised you the canned goods?"

"Lesquallan, Ltd."

"Oh, Lord!" said Swenson. "An outfit that expects lions to lie down with lambs!"

The red *ship-calling* light flashed on.

"Number 4 to dispatcher. This is Captain Elsing. Dovorkin...."

"Dispatcher to Number 4. Dovorkin, hell. This is Swenson. What blasts?"

"B jet just went out. Atomic slug clogged."

"How radioactive is the spout?" asked Swenson.

"Heavy."

"Have somebody who's already had a family put on armor and clean up the mess," Swenson said, "and alter course for Luna City. I'll send you the exact course in a few minutes. When you get to Luna, land beside the Moulton Trust's ship. Now stand by to record code."

Swenson reached back to Mister Cerobie. "Acme private code book."

Silently, the Chairman of the Board handed it to him. When Swenson had finished coding, he handed the original message to Mister Cerobie. The message read:

"Captain Elsing, have crew start fight with Moulton's crew. Not much incentive will be necessary. See that no real damage is done. Urgent. Will take all responsibility. Explain later. Cerobie."

"Swenson," Mister Cerobie said quietly, "you *are* insane. Tear that up."

With slow dignity, Swenson put on his coat. He stood there, smiling, and looking at Mister Cerobie. The memory of Dovorkin stalked unpleasantly through the

Chairman's mind. Everything was hopeless, anyway. Better go out with a bang than a whimper.

"All right, send it," he said. "There is plenty of time to countermand—after I talk to you."

When Swenson had finished sending the coded message, he turned back to Mister Cerobie. "What's this I hear from Dovorkin about a Senator being aboard Number 7 at Luna?"

A member of the Board began: "After all...."

Mister Cerobie cut him off: "Your information is correct, Swenson. A Senator has shipped with us. However, I would prefer to discuss the matter in my private office."

Swenson crossed the room to the astrographer in the calculating booth and said: "Plot the free-falling curve for Number 5 to Mars." Then he followed Mister Cerobie into the Chairman's office.

Half an hour later, they came out and Swenson went back to his desk. First he glanced at the free-falling plot. Then he snorted, called the astrographer and fired him. Next he said to Mister Cerobie: "Is that half load of snuff...."

"Yes, it is. You know Martians as well as I do. With their type of nose, they must get quite a sensation. I understand they go a bit berserk. That's why their government outlaws snuff as an Earth vice. However, our cargo release states that it is being sent for 'medicinal purposes.' It's no consequence to us what they use the snuff for. We're just hauling it. And I don't have to tell you how fantastic a rate we're getting."

"To hell with the canned goods part of the load," Swenson said. "Can you get a full haul of snuff?"

"Possibly. But it would cost."

"Even this outfit can afford to grease palms."

"I'll see what I can do."

"What's the Senator on the Moon for?"

"He's supposed to make a speech on Conquest Day." Mister Cerobie lit a cigar. "That's day after tomorrow," he added.

"Exactly where is this eloquence to be expounded?"

"The Senator is speaking at the dedication of the new underground recreation dome. It's just outside Luna City. They've bored a tunnel from the main dome cluster. This dedication is considered very important. Everybody in Luna will be there. It's been declared an official holiday, with all crews released. Even the maintenance and public service personnel have been cut to skeleton staffs."

"With that fiesta scheduled on our beloved satellite," said Swenson, "we won't have to worry about getting the Senator off for some time. His name's Higby, isn't it?" Mister Cerobie nodded. "Then he'll whoop it up long enough for you to get that demurrage mess straightened out."

"Unfortunately, it isn't that simple. The Senator is due for another speech on Mars. The timing is close— he only has a minimum of leeway. As you mentioned, Number 7 is grounded for demurrage. And we can't ship the Senator out on Number 4 because of the bad jet."

Swenson was silent for a long time. The beer gurgled pleasantly as he drank it. Then a bright smile—which could have been due either to inspiration or beer—spread across his face.

"If that idiot Dovorkin can be trusted," he said, "the Senator is speaking in the early afternoon, our time. Do you happen to know just when he starts yapping? And the scheduled length of the spiel?"

"I'll check it." Mister Cerobie turned to one of his assistants. Swenson took down the *Luna Data Handbook* and thumbed through it.

A moment later, the assistant handed a slip of paper to the Board Chairman.

"The Senator," Mister Cerobie said, "will speak from 1300 hours to 1500 hours."

Swenson smiled and stuck a marker in the *Luna Data Handbook*.

"Now," he said, "about this snuff. Can you have it loaded by tomorrow night?"

"I don't see how."

"Remember our agreement in the office. If we don't do something, we're through, so all we can do is lose. Leave me be and don't ask questions. I want to blast Number 2 into low Earth-orbital tomorrow night."

Mister Cerobie looked off into that nowhere which was the daily destiny of Acme. "All right," he said, "I was born a damn fool. I'll do my best to have a full load of snuff aboard—somehow—tomorrow night."

Swenson went back to his Dispatch Sheet. During the next five hours, he looked up only long enough to order another case of beer and a new astrographer.

Finally, he called Heilberg, the assistant dispatcher who was on the night shift, gave him a lecture concerning dispatching in general and the present situation in particular, promoted a date with one of the stenographers, and departed.

• • •

Vocabulary words:
Find these words in the section, write the sentence they are used in, and write your own definition. If you are stuck, look it up in the dictionary, but still write a definition in your own words.

countermand
spiel

Comprehension/extension questions:

Which do you suppose was easier to order, the beer or the astrographer?

Why did Swenson recommend a full load of snuff instead of half and half with canned goods?

• • •

When Swenson came back the next morning, he was sober, ornery and disinclined to do any work. He cornered O'Toole, the labor relations man, and began talking women. O'Toole was intrigued but evasive.

"Your trouble," Swenson said, "is not with women. It's with evolution. I don't blame evolution for creating women. I blame it for abandoning the egg. Just when it had invented a reasonable method of reproduction which didn't make the female silly-looking and tie her down needlessly for nine months...."

"I don't think they're silly-looking."

"Maybe you don't, O'Toole, but I do. And you must admit that nine months is a hell of a long time to fool around with something that could be hatched in an incubator under automatic controls. Look at the times saving. If evolution hadn't abandoned the egg idea, half the human race wouldn't waste time being damned incubators."

O'Toole backed away. He had never heard the legend of Swenson's egg speech.

"Don't tell me," Swenson went on, "that evolution is efficient. Are you married, O'Toole?"

"Yes, I—"

"Wouldn't you rather your wife laid an egg than—"

"I don't know," O'Toole interrupted, "but I do know that I'd like to find out what the dispatch situation is at the moment."

Swenson grabbed a piece of paper and drew a diagram.

While O'Toole was studying the diagram, someone laid a Special Message on Swenson's desk. Swenson glanced at it:

Acme Interplanetary Express
147 Z Street
New York

Your ship Number 4 is hereby grounded at Luna City, pending an investigation of a riot involving your men, and for non-payment of bill for atomic slug purification. Your Number 4 is also charged with unpaid demurrage bill.

Planetary Commerce Commission

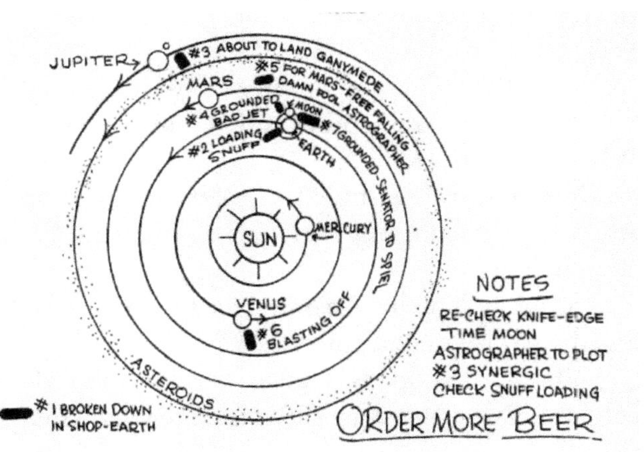

Swenson muttered: "Good!" and threw the Special Message in the wastebasket. Mister Cerobie, who had just entered the office, fished the form out and read it.

"It never rains, but it pours," he said.

"You can't stand long on one foot," Swenson answered without looking up. "Put all your troubles in one basket and then lose the basket. *Morituri te salutamus.* Have you heard my theory about the advantage of reproduction via the egg? And get me a beer."

"I will get you a beer, but if you say a word about that egg theory, I will fire you. I heard you talking to O'Toole."

"Okay. We'll forget the egg for the nonce. Did you pilfer that snuff?"

"It's being loaded. And it cost Acme—"

"Did you expect it would fall like manna from heaven?" Swenson flipped the switch of the intercom to Acme's launching area. "Give me Number 2. Captain Wilkins."

"What are you going to do?" Mister Cerobie asked.

"Don't you remember what I told you yesterday? Where's that beer?"

Mister Cerobie smiled, a weary, dogged smile, the smile of a man who had bet on drawing to a belly straight.[4]

"Captain Wilkins," came over the intercom, "calling Swenson, dispatcher, for orders."

"Blast as soon as loaded for low altitude Earth-orbital." Swenson was silent a moment, then: "Hell,

---

[4] a belly straight or belly buster is four cards of a five-card straight, where the player is missing one of the middle cards. Such as 7-9-10-J.

don't you know the plot? All right, I'll give it to you. Full jets, two minutes, azimuth....[5]."

Mister Cerobie interrupted quietly: "Swenson, don't you think you'd better check with the astrographer?"

Turning off the intercom, Swenson spun in his chair. "Any decent dispatcher knows that one by heart. So maybe I'm wrong. Then Number 2 will pile up on either the Moon or the Earth. If that happens, you can collect the insurance and get out of this mess." He flipped on the intercom switch. "Sorry, Captain Wilkins, brass interference. As I was saying, azimuth...."

Mister Cerobie made no effort to continue the conversation. He was reading an astrogram, which had just been handed to him.

Acme Interplanetary Express
147 Z Street
New York
Earth

Hear persistent rumor your ship on which I am a passenger held here for non-payment of demurrage. Must make world crisis speech on mars as scheduled. Astrogram truth of situation at once. Investigation of such matters now pending before subcommittee. Do not astrogram collect.

---

[5] angle between the north vector and the perpendicular projection of the object down onto the horizon

SWENSON, DISPATCHER

Sen. Hiram C. Higby

Swenson snapped off the intercom, glanced at his Dispatch Sheet, leaned back in his chair and closed his eyes. He was silent for the next half hour and drank three beers, looking either thoughtful or asleep. Mister Cerobie smoked a cigar until it burned his mustache.

When the third beer was finished, Swenson reached for an astrogram blank and wrote:

Hon. Senator Hiram C. Higby Esq.
Acme Interplanetary Express
Luna City

Rumor re unpaid demurrage utterly unfounded. Information here that rumor started by your opposition. Have vital new data for your Luna city speech. Will send speech insert at once.

James Cerobie

Mister Cerobie, who had been reading over Swenson's shoulder, said: "You know that demurrage rumor is true."

"If things don't work out and we have any trouble, you can say you hadn't heard about the demurrage. By the way, can you write an insert to a political speech?"

"I suppose so. I've lied before."

"Make sure it will take ten minutes to deliver—even talking fast—which Senators don't usually do."

"What," inquired Mister Cerobie, "shall I write about?"

"You know that scandal Senator Higby's opposition just got involved in. That business about slave labor exploitation on Venus. The story broke this morning. Get in touch with my friend Max Zempky on Telenews and have him give you some inside details. It doesn't matter if they're important or not. The Senator will grab anything that might pep up his speech. Besides, he's probably been having a large time in Luna City and hasn't heard about this morning's story."

Mister Cerobie executed a sweeping bow. "Yes, sir. And if this thing doesn't work, I told you yesterday in my office what would happen."

Swenson shrugged. "Kismet."

As Mister Cerobie opened the door to his private office, Swenson called after him: "Where's this outfit's attorney?"

"In the Board Room."

"Find him and send him in here."

Mister Cerobie nodded.

"And," Swenson added, "be damned sure that speech insert will run at least ten minutes. More, if possible."

Mister Cerobie slammed the door.

Five minutes later, slim, soft-spoken Van Euing, Acme's attorney, coughed behind the dispatcher's chair. Swenson swiveled from coding the astrogram and dropped his cigarette. "What the hell—oh, you. Lawyers are like policemen—they sneak up on people."

"How did you know I was the firm's attorney?"

"I watched you try that unfair-trade-practice suit against Lesquallan Ltd. two years ago. It was snowing outside. I was broke and the courtroom was warm. You should have won the case. Some of their evidence looked phony to me. Anyway, you did a good job."

"Thank you."

"Did you ever stop to think about the advantage of the egg—"

"Mister Cerobie said you wished to speak to me."

"That's right. I want you to draw up a something-or-other—you know what I mean—grounding Moulton Trust's ship on the Moon until this fight hassle is settled."

"You mean you wish me to prepare a restraining order?"

"Restrain, yeah! And restrain them as long as you can. I wish you could restrain them forever. This solar system would be a better place."

"On what grounds am I to base my order?"

"Claim they started the fight and our crew's so bashed up that we haven't enough able men to blast off."

"But I'm afraid we can't prove that."

"And what's it going to cost us to try? You're on retainer. The total bill for said restraining order will be only the price of some legal paper and the services of a notary. The steno's hired by the month, like you."

Van Euing looked puzzled. "What good will it do?"

"You know how long it takes courts to do anything. Before your order is tossed out, Moulton will have been grounded for a week."

Van Euing lit his pipe. "In legal parlance, it is something irregular, which, being translated, means it's a slick trick."

"All it's going to cost *you* is being half an hour late to lunch."

Van Euing puffed a moment on his pipe and said: "Because of your audacity, Swenson, and furthermore, because you'll be fired tomorrow, I'll prepare the restraining order."

Swenson put out his hand and his blunt fingers closed around Van Euing's delicate ones.

When Van Euing had gone, Swenson returned to coding the astrogram. He checked the form twice and sent it.

• • •

Vocabulary words:
Find these words in the section, write the sentence they are used in, and write your own definition. If you are stuck, look it up in the dictionary, but still write a definition in your own words.

incubators
nonce
kismet
audacity

Comprehension/extension questions:

Is Swenson brilliant or inept?

What is the egg theory?

• • •

Then he turned over his desk to an apprentice dispatcher, left orders to be called if anything broke down, and went out to lunch.

It was 2:30 P.M. when news of the restraining order arrived in the quiet, streamlined offices of the Moulton Trust. Two minutes later, the offices were still streamlined, but not quiet.

The three major stockholders of the great organization, N. Rovance, F. K. Esrov, and Cecil Neinfort-Whritings, formed a tiny huddle at one end of the long conference table. Esrov was waving a copy of the order.

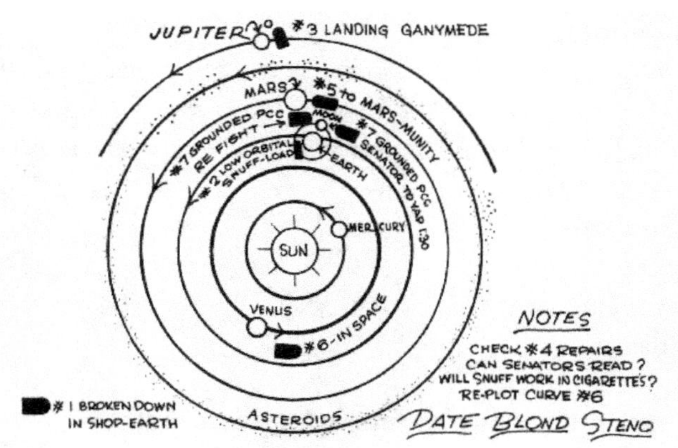

"Gentlemen, we can consider this nothing but an outrage!"

"Blackmail, really!" It was Neinfort-Whritings's lisping voice.

"Whatever it is, this sort of nonsense must be stopped at the beginning. It might set a precedent."

"May I suggest," Rovance broke in, "that, as the matter of precedent is sure to arise, we take no action without first consulting Lesquallan Ltd."

"An excellent idea," Esrov nodded. He switched on the intercom to his first secretary. "Connect me with Lesquallan Ltd. I want to speak with Novell Lesquallan. Inform him that it is urgent."

"He just entered our office." The voice that came from the intercom carried the slightest trace of surprise. "He said he desired to discuss something about canned goods and snuff. I shall send him in at once."

Rovance turned to Neinfort-Whritings. "I fear that old Cerobie is becoming senile. Apparently he has lost his mind."

"But really, did he ever have one?"

Nobody laughed. Esrov slammed the restraining order on the conference table and stood up. "Gentlemen, what shall we do concerning—"

"Yes, gentlemen, that is just what I want to know."

Three heads pivoted. Novell Lesquallan, sole owner of Lesquallan Ltd., stood in the doorway. He was a broad, ruddy-faced man with a voice trained to basso interruptions.

"I understand, Mr. Lesquallan," Esrov said, "that you have a matter to discuss with us."

"Yes! Sit down, F.K. We have some talking to do— about that bankrupt, dishonest Acme Interplanetary Express."

"Quite a coincidence," Neinfort-Whritings murmured.

"You got trouble with that outfit, too? That settles it. They've cluttered up the orderly progress of free enterprise long enough. Out they go."

Novell Lesquallan swiftly read the document and bellowed an unintelligible remark.

"Something, quite," Neinfort-Whritings agreed.

Lesquallan got his voice under control. "What action do you intend to take?"

"We hadn't decided," Rovance answered. "We received the order only a few minutes ago."

"Before we form our plans," Esrov said, "we would like some information about your problems with Acme. We understand it involves canned goods and snuff."

"Yes, those damned…. At the last minute, they turned down a small load of canned goods for Luna that we'd been decent enough to give them at reduced rates. They can't get away with that kind of thing long. But that's just the beginning. They got hold of the contract and permit to haul a consignment of medicinal snuff to Mars. We had already arranged for that cargo. You know that snuff situation. Through certain contacts, we have been able—perfectly legally—to have permits issued. That customs man must have taken a double—"

"We understand," Rovance broke in. "We have had occasion to make similar arrangements. The rates—and other inducements—are extremely satisfactory."

"Well, gentlemen," Lesquallan demanded, "what are we going to do about this unprecedented situation?"

"I suggest," Neinfort-Whritings said, "that we have our legal staffs meet in joint session. We should impress on them that the quashing of this restraining order is urgent. Perhaps we should consider debts owed us by the judiciary we helped elect."

"An excellent idea," Lesquallan declared. "I will take care of that part of it myself, personally."

"As to the snuff matter," Esrov said, "I think we should emphasize to our mutual contact that he should be more discriminating in issuing permits."

"That's all right for now," Lesquallan snapped. "But he's done with, too. I'll see to it that he's replaced."

"As to the canned goods situation," Rovance said, "it seems to me that we should have a subsidiary company to handle our excess cargoes—at reduced rates, of course. It shouldn't cost too much to pick up one of the less financially secure companies—such as Acme."

Esrov nodded. "An excellent idea."

"I agree," Lesquallan said and sat down. "But first we must dispose of today's damned annoyances. I suggest that we outline a plan for immediate action."

"To begin with," Esrov reminded him, "we must deal with the restraining order."

• • •

Vocabulary words:

Find these words in the section, write the sentence they are used in, and write your own definition. If you are stuck, look it up in the dictionary, but still write a definition in your own words.

precedent
basso

Comprehension/extension questions:

What is the plan for dealing with Acme Interplanetary
Express?

• • •

When Swenson came back from lunch, he was not
as sober and thus in a better mood. Mister Cerobie's
insert to the Senator's speech was on his desk. Swenson
read the first few lines:

As a further indication of the methods, devices,
malfeasances, and corrupt practices employed,
used, and sustained by those with whom you have
called upon me to negotiate in the highest tribunal
in Washington, let me cite the following
information which I have just received. Although
this information is top-drawer, restricted and
highly secret, I was able to obtain it through certain
channels which, as a man of honor, I must leave
undisclosed.

The right of all creatures to be free is a
fundamental, an inviolable, right and yet on
Venus....

Swenson said to himself: "Mister Cerobie is in the
wrong business," and started coding the insert. He had
almost finished when the ship-calling light flashed red.

"Number 5 to Dispatcher. Captain Verbold
speaking."

"Dispatcher to Number 5. This is Swenson. Go ahead."

"I'm afraid you can't help me. May I speak to Mister Cerobie?"

"He's out to lunch."

"This matter is serious. I am faced with what amounts to mutiny."

"Sorry, but I got troubles, too. Maybe I can find Mister Cerobie, maybe I can't. Why don't you tell me your grief?"

Captain Verbold hesitated. "It's something I've been expecting. The crew has stated that they will leave the ship at Mars." Captain Verbold's next sentence was pronounced word by word in code. "I even have private information that there is a plot to take over the ship and blast directly to Earth, where the crew feel their case can be more justly presented."

"What are they squawking about?"

"Everything. Wages have not been paid for six months. Poor radiation shielding. Food not up to standard. You know the story."

"It's not the first time I've heard it."

"What am I to do?"

"First, read them section 942 in your copy of *Space Regulations*," said Swenson. "If they divert ship from Mars without your permission, it's mutiny. That means the neutron death chamber or, if they are very lucky, life sentences to the Luna Penal Colony. Get them all together and read it to them. You're free-falling now, so even the jetters won't have to be on duty."

"But if I could talk to Mister Cerobie—"

"I've already told you I don't know where the hell he is. He couldn't do you any good, anyway. Didn't you ever read *Space Regulations*? Section 19: 'The captain of a ship in flight is *solely responsible* for the maintenance of discipline and his orders cannot be changed or overruled'."

"Swenson, you said a moment ago that this was your first suggestion. I presume, therefore, that you have others."

"I have two others." Swenson paused long enough for a brief study of his Master Ship Location Chart, which he had just brought up to date. The chart showed the position of all ships at the moment in space. "There's a patrol cruiser loaded with gendarmes three million miles behind you on a course paralleling yours. It's one of the new Arrow Class and if they blast full, they can catch you in ten hours. Mention to the crew that you could notify the police boys and have them pick you up and escort you to Mars."

"What is the patrol ship's number and call letters?"

"Arrow—British—Earth—number 96. Call letters MMXAH."

"Thanks. If things get too bad, I might take advantage of our valiant guarders of the spaceways. All right, you said you had three suggestions. What's the third?"

"Some goons on a Moulton Trust ship, parked beside our number 2 on the Moon, started a fight and beat up our boys. We're about to sue Moulton for plenty. Tell your crew about it and suggest that if they behave, we'll cut them in on the proceeds from the suit, in addition to paying their wages as soon as a snuff cargo that I had to send into orbital gets to Mars."

"On whose authority am I to make such a statement?"

"Swenson's. You don't need any other, do you? I know most of the boys on your mobile junkyard. They trust me, so they'll trust you. You have my word that Cerobie will go for the idea."

"You talk to Cerobie and let me know what happens. Meanwhile, I'll think over your suggestions."

The ship-calling light blinked off and Swenson went back to coding the speech insert.

As he was finishing, O'Toole came in.

Swenson looked up. "O'Toole, sure and it's one hell of a job you're doing. You've got me in a fight with myself. My Swedish half wants to ignore you and my Irish half wants to punch you in the nose. You're supposed to handle labor relations. And I just received a message from Captain Verbold of Number 5 that his crew is about to mutiny."

"Mother of God, what can I do?" cried O'Toole. "This outfit's so broke, it doesn't have enough money to pay the filing fee for bankruptcy."

"In the face of adversity, you should spit."

"Who are you quoting?"

"Me."

"Look, Swenson, I'm supposed to supervise labor relations, sure. Labor is something you hire. That's done by paying wages—on time."

"At least you should have brains enough to understand the advantage of the egg."

"What?" asked O'Toole blankly.

"I've already explained it to you. Apparently it didn't get past your hair. I shall therefore make a second attempt. Do you understand the principle of the egg?"

"I don't—"

"Of course not. You never stopped to analyze it. You just assumed that because human beings are born the way they are, it is the best method. How much pain and trouble does a hen have laying an egg? Does she—"

"Getting back to number 5," O'Toole said firmly, "what did Captain Verbold—"

"Consider the advantage of the egg from another angle, O'Toole. Let's say your wife lays an egg and, at the moment, you don't have money enough to support another child. All you would have to do is put the egg in cold storage until your ship comes in. Then you can take the egg out and incubate it. Instead of being—"

The click of the latch as O'Toole closed the door caused Swenson to spin in his chair. Tossing his pencil on the Dispatch Sheet, he put on his coat and went home.

• • •

Vocabulary words:

Find these words in the section, write the sentence they are used in, and write your own definition. If you are stuck, look it up in the dictionary, but still write a definition in your own words.

malfeasances
inviolable

Comprehension/extension questions:

How would you describe Swenson? How do his boss and coworkers see him?

• • •

When the dispatcher for Acme Interplanetary Express arrived at the office the following morning, a Special Message lay in sublime isolation on his desk. Swenson opened a beer and read the message.

Board of Directors
Acme Interplanetary Express

Gentlemen:

Your restraining order concerning our ship at Luna City can only be considered as representing a warped and intolerable concept of justice. We will take every legal action available to us.

Moreover, your action in refusing, without notice, a load which we were so kind as to offer you and your immoral dealings in contraband snuff force us to sever all commercial relations with your organization.

We are taking appropriate action with the Planetary Commerce Commission.

SWENSON, DISPATCHER

Yours sincerely,
Moulton Trust
Lesquallan Ltd.

Swenson was smiling cherubically and bringing his Master Chart up to date when O'Toole came in.

"Swenson, did you have eggs for breakfast? And how goes with the dispatch?"

Carefully noting the last change of ship position on the Master Chart, Swenson turned to O'Toole.

"Things are like so," he said, and drew a diagram.

While O'Toole was studying the diagram, Swenson placed a call to Moulton Trust. "Give me Esrov. Yes, Esrov himself. This is Swenson, Acme Interplanetary. If Esrov doesn't want to talk to me, jets to him, but I think I have some information he can use."

"Will you please hold on, Mr. Swenson? I will convey your message."

Swenson looked at O'Toole for a moment in silence. "No, I don't like eggs for eating. My theory concerns another aspect—"

"I know," said O'Toole resignedly.

Esrov's urbane voice came from the desk speaker. "Mr. Swenson, you have some information for us?"

"Yes, Esrov. I've just seen your message to our Board and I want you to know that I can certainly understand your position. I could not prevent the restraining order. However, I have a suggestion as to what you can do about it."

"We are doing everything we can."

"Didn't you support Senator Higby for re-election last year? Well, he has shipped with us on an inspection tour of planetary outposts. Right now, he's on the Moon and will speak at 1:30 this afternoon at the official opening of the new Recreation Center. It occurred to me that it might be worthwhile for you to send him a message suggesting that he incorporate in his speech something about the laxity of the Planetary Commerce Commission that allowed you to get into this mess."

"An excellent idea, Mr. Swenson. We shall give it immediate consideration. And, by the way, if for any reason your employment with Acme should terminate, we should be able to find a suitable position for you with our company."

"Thanks, Esrov." Swenson switched off the set.

"You dirty, stinking," O'Toole blared, "doublecrossing—"

"Calm down, O'Toole. Don't get off the rocket until she's on the ground. I've got reasons."

"Reasons? You haven't even got *reason*! And you're a crook!"

"Now don't let my Irish half get on top. I want that Senator to talk as long as possible. Let's go back to the egg."

"You've laid it."

"For the last time, let me explain. If evolution had followed my theory, I, being a man, would not lay eggs. Women would and therefore they would escape—"

"Swenson," Mister Cerobie called from the door of the Board Room, "you are hired—tentatively—as a dispatcher, not an egg-evolution theorist. Now come in here. The Board wants to talk to you."

Swenson jerked the diagram out of O'Toole's hand and followed Cerobie.

Ten minutes later, he came out of the Board Room, saying: "Gentlemen, the Senator speaks at 1:30 this afternoon. At 6:00 either fire me, crucify me and make me drink boiled beer alone, or give me a raise."

* * *

Vocabulary words:
Find these words in the section, write the sentence they are used in, and write your own definition. If you are stuck, look it up in the dictionary, but still write a definition in your own words.

contraband
cherubically
urbane
reason

Comprehension/extension questions:

Why does Swenson want the Senator to speak at such length? What is the advantage to Acme?

* * *

The clock on the wall over the dispatcher's desk showed 2:59 when Swenson called Acme's Luna City Terminal. "Dispatcher to Numbers 7 and 4, have crew stand by to blast off in exactly 15 minutes. I don't give a damn about regulations or the P.C.C. This is an order from your company. It must be obeyed. Number 7 will follow course as originally planned—destination Mars. Number 4 will blast for Earth, curve to be given in space."

Fifteen minutes later, the dispatcher's office at Acme Interplanetary Express was quieter than an abandoned and forgotten tomb. The Board of Directors stood silently in a semi-circle behind Swenson. Every employee, even the stenographers, were jammed into the frowsy room.

As the hand of the clock sliced off the last second of the 15 minutes, Swenson looked over his shoulder—and laughed, a great, resounding laugh. Then he flicked the switch and picked up the microphone.

"Swenson dispatcher to 7 and 4. Blast! Over. Swenson dispatcher to 4 and 7. Blast!"

Suddenly the silent room was filled with the roar of the jets as they thundered in the imaginations of the men and women crowded around the dispatcher's desk. The tension broke as almost a sob of gladness. What if it proved a hopeless dream, a mere stalling of inevitable ruin? They were no longer grounded. They were in space.

To those in the room, it seemed only an instant until the ship-calling light flashed on. "Number 7 to dispatcher. In space. All clear."

"Dispatcher to Number 7, steady as she goes."

The red light was off for a moment. Then: "Number 4 to dispatcher. In space. All clear."

"Dispatcher to Number 4. Temporary curve A 17. Will send exact curve plot in half an hour." Swenson turned to the astrographer. "Give me a plot for Chicago. I don't want to land her in this state. Just a matter of prudence. She's registered in this state."

The astrographer shouldered his way through the crowd. When he reached the calculators, his swift fingers began pushing buttons. Swenson leaned back.

"Mischief, thou art a'space," he said. "Now take whatever course thou wilt."

At 3:30, Swenson reached again for the microphone. "Dispatcher to Number 2. You are circling Earth at low orbital. Decelerate and drop to

stratosphere. Maintain position over New York. Curve and blasting data...."

At 4:00, he called Max Zempky at *Telenews*. "Anything frying at Luna?"

"My God, yes! Senator Higby yapped sixteen minutes overtime and the shadow knife-edge caught everybody with their air tanks down. The control crews were listening to the speech and there wasn't anybody left to switch over the heating-cooling system. You've been to the Moon, so you know what happens. When day changes to night and you haven't got any atmosphere, the temperature drops from boiling to practically absolute zero. Sure, the automatic controls worked, but there wasn't any crew to adjust and service the heaters and coolers. It's a mess. Say, haven't you got a ship or two up there?"

"I got 'em out in time."

"Well, Moulton didn't. Their ship's been considerably damaged."

"Thanks, Max. Let me know if anything else breaks."

While Swenson had been talking, two Special Messages and an astrogram had been laid on his desk. He first read one of the Special Messages.

Acme Interplanetary Express
147 Z Street
New York

Gentlemen:

We are holding you responsible for the damage to our ship Number 57, now on the Moon. The captain of your ship should have known the potential danger and warned Senator Higby of the time factor.

We will contact the PCC at once.

F. K. Esrov
Moulton Trust

Swenson scribbled an answer and handed it to an assistant.

Moulton Trust

Nuts, Esrov. You've got to think up something better than that. We have no control over public officials, except during flight. Bellyache all you want to the PCC.

Sedately,
Swenson

The astrogram was from Senator Hiram C. Higby:
My being stranded on moon unmitigated and unparalleled outrage. Must speak as scheduled on mars. Find me transportation. Will deal later with your company concerning infamous treatment.

Sen. Hiram C. Higby

Swenson replied:

Unfortunate circumstance unavoidable. Your speech magnificent. Will make every effort to secure immediate transportation to mars.

Swenson

• • •

Vocabulary words:
Find these words in the section, write the sentence they are used in, and write your own definition. If you are stuck, look it up in the dictionary, but still write a definition in your own words.

frowsy
stratosphere
unmitigated

Comprehension/extension questions:

What was the consequence of the Senator speaking too long?

Is this positive or negative to Acme?

• • •

The second Special Message was from the PCC and asked with crisp and blunt formality why two Acme ships, which had been officially grounded by the Commission, had blasted off the Moon.

In answer, Swenson was mild and apologetic. What else could he have done? Surely the Commission must understand that his first duty was to save his ships from damage. He had been informed by his captains that the shadow knife-edge was almost due, and there was no possibility of the control crews servicing the temperature-change compensators in time. It was an emergency. The matter of the grounding could be settled later.

When his answer was finished, he coded it, along with the Special Message from Moulton Trust, the astrogram from Senator Higby, and his replies. Finally, he coded the Special Message from PCC.

Then he called Number 5.

"Number 5 to dispatcher. This is Verbold. What goes on now?"

"You tell me. Dwelleth thy household in peace?"

"For the moment."

"Have you followed my instructions?"

"In general, yes."

"Did your crew hear Senator Higby's speech?"

"Most of them. What else is there to do in this rat-trap?"

"I could think of a lot of things. But as long as the crew heard the Honorable's spiel, that's all that matters. Do you know about the little affair half an hour ago at Luna City?"

"No."

"Check your news recorder. Have the item broadcast to the crew. Then decode the sequence of messages I'm about to send and read them—at your discretion—to the men. Stand by to record code."

When he had finished, Swenson leaned back and opened a beer. "All we can do now is wait. But I'd give my grandmother's immortal soul, if the old shrew had one, to be in the sacred sanctum of Moulton Trust."

Lesquallan sat on the edge of the long table in Moulton's Board Room. He spoke slowly and for once his voice was low:

"Esrov, did you or did you not suggest to our Senator Higby that he lengthen his speech on the Moon to include certain new information? And did that information involve my company along with yours?"

"Mr. Lesquallan, the matter concerns only a minor aspect of policy," said Esrov placatingly.

"Minor aspect of policy, hell! It concerns business. Look what happened at Luna. And you let us get publicly involved in it. Such matters must never be handled openly."

Esrov did not answer.

"Did you send such a message, Rovance?" Rovance shook his head. Lesquallan turned to Neinfort-Whritings. "Did you?"

"No, Lesquallan." Neinfort-Whritings gently pulled a Special Message form from beneath Esrov's folded hands as they lay on the gleaming conference table.

Lesquallan swung back to Esrov. "Did *you* send it?"

Esrov looked down at his folded hands At last he said quietly: "Yes, I sent a message to the Senator—in our mutual interests."

"Was it your own idea? Or did someone else suggest it?"

"The basic thought came from a most unexpected source. It was, we might say, one of those happy breaks of industry. The dispatcher at Acme had the sense to cooperate with us. He gave me certain otherwise unavailable information, and—"

"What was his name?"

"I don't—oh, yes, it was Swenson."

"You… you fool… *idiot*!"

Neinfort-Whritings handed Lesquallan the Special Message he had taken from Esrov. It was the one from Swenson, which began: "Nuts, Esrov."

Lesquallan read the message. Then he said slowly: "I've dealt with that clown Swenson before—over minor matters. I never thought he had that much brains." He looked at Esrov. "Or insight. Swenson's a smart man. Therefore, he must be eliminated."

"I still maintain," Rovance said, "that the basis of the matter is the strangling of free enterprise."

"I agree," said Lesquallan. "What right has Acme to interfere with free enterprise? They haven't a dollar to our million."

"What shall we do?" Neinfort-Whritings murmured.

"Follow Swenson's suggestion. We're going to the PCC—and we're going to our top contacts. They owe us plenty."

"Shall we dictate a memo?" Esrov put in.

"Call the PCC," Lesquallan ordered. "We're not dictating anything. And we're not sending any messages to anybody. Let the PCC send them!"

No employee of Acme Interplanetary Express had left the smoke-dense office when the ship-calling light went on: "Number 5 to Swenson. Verbold speaking."

"Dispatcher to Number 5. Go ahead."

"Uproar under control. I followed your instructions. A crew that's laughing won't mutiny. The crew sends thanks and their most pious wishes for the distress of Moulton. The men expect shares of the proceeds, if any, in the lawsuit. But they insist on being paid on Mars."

"They will be, Captain Verbold. Now I've got to keep this beam clear. Good luck." Swenson turned to Mister Cerobie. "I presume you can at least find enough cash for the back pay?"

Mister Cerobie did not answer. He was staring at a Special Message which had just been handed to him. He dropped it on Swenson's desk.

Acme Interplanetary Express
147 Z Street
New York

Because of your violation of Space Regulations and unprecedented effrontery, your ships Numbers 7 and 4 are hereby ordered to return to the Moon. There they will be impounded. A police patrol escort has been dispatched to insure your compliance with our order.

Planetary Commerce Commission

Swenson read the message and looked up.
"Well?" asked Mister Cerobie.

The murmur of voices died. The dispatcher's office of Acme Interplanetary Express was a silent, isolated world. Swenson wrote an astrogram and handed it to the Chairman of the Board.

"Shall I code it?"

Mister Cerobie read the astrogram. He read it a second time and his perplexity vanished.

"But will it work?" he asked.

Swenson shrugged. "It ought to. Remember what happened when Solar System Freight lost that chemical load? We're stratosphering over New York. Anyway, he wouldn't dare take the chance. Shall I code it, Mister Cerobie?"

"Absolutely!"

The men and women of Acme crowded and squirmed for a look at the astrogram on Swenson's desk. O'Toole realized first and yelled. Slowly, as understanding came, other voices took it up, until the office was a chaos of sound. Bottles appeared from nowhere. O'Toole raised one of them: "Sure and St. Patrick would have loved it!"

Calmly, Swenson coded:

Senator Hiram C. Higby
Acme Interplanetary Express
Luna City

Only transportation available our ship now in earth stratosphere above New York with cargo snuff. Will dispatch this ship special to moon for your disposal. However must jettison cargo to lighten ship. Will notify Air Pollution and PCC. Only alternative complete clearance by PCC our ships numbers 7 and 4. Will then dispatch one of them to pick you up. Order to jettison will be given in half an hour unless we receive word from you. Have you any influence with the PCC? Send reaction at once. Urgency obvious.

Swenson

The dispatcher for Acme said to himself: "I doubt very seriously if any sane Senator up for re-election would want the official records to show that, because he talked too long on the Moon, a cargo of snuff was dumped over New York. Sneezing voters cannot see a candidate's name on ballot."

Twenty minutes later, the replying astrogram was in Swenson's hand.

Acme interplanetary express
147 Z Street
New York
Earth

Order clearing your ships 7 and 4 approved by PCC. Have ship immediately reverse course and pick me up. Under no circumstances jettison snuff. Send further information concerning slave labor exploitation Venus for inclusion in my forthcoming mars speech. Have speech insert in same form as before.

SWENSON, DISPATCHER

Senator Hiram C. Higby

"And that, Mister Cerobie," said Swenson, "is how you slide out of a jam. You'll get enough cash for that snuff haul to Mars to pay the crew of Number 5 when she lands there. And you'll have enough left over to pay the demurrage and repair charges at Luna. Now open me a beer."

Mister Cerobie opened the beer wearily.

"You're fired, Swenson," he said. "I'll be damned if I'll write another speech or be your bartender."

Swenson drank and smiled.

The ship-calling light flashed red. "Number 3 to dispatcher. This is Captain Marwovan. Compartment holed by meteorite. Cannot land on Ganymede until we make repairs. Send me the orbital curve so we can circle until the hole is patched. And tell Mister Cerobie that the crew is complaining about back pay."

Transferring the beer to his other hand, Swenson grabbed the microphone. "Dispatcher to Number 3...."

• • •

Vocabulary words:
Find these words in the section, write the sentence they are used in, and write your own definition. If you are stuck, look it up in the dictionary, but still write a definition in your own words.

pious
jettison

exploitation
Comprehension/extension questions:

How did Swenson get Moulton to shoot themselves in the foot?

Why did the Senator agree to clear the Acme ships for flight?

Will Swenson really be fired?

Swenson, Dispatcher, by R. DeWitt Miller, Published April 1956

R. DeWitt Miller was born in California January 22, 2910 and died June 3, 1958. He wrote two novels and several short fiction and nonfiction works from the 1930s to 1950s.

PRIME DIFFERENCE

By ALAN E. NOURSE
Illustrated by SCHOENHEER

*Being two men rolled out of one would solve
my problems—but which one would I be?*

I suppose that every guy reaches a point once in his lifetime when he gets one hundred and forty percent fed up with his wife.

Understand now—I've got nothing against marriage or any thing like that. Marriage is great. It's a good old red-blooded American Institution. Except that it's got one defect in it big enough to throw a cat through, especially when you happen to be married to a woman like Marge—

It's so *permanent.*

Oh, I'd have divorced Marge in a minute if we'd been living in the Blissful 'Fifties—but with the Family Solidarity Amendment of 1968, and all the divorce taxes we have these days since the women got their teeth into politics, to say nothing of the Aggrieved Spouse

Compensation Act, I'd have been a pauper for the rest of my life if I'd tried it. That's aside from the social repercussions involved.

You can't really blame me for looking for another way out. But a man has to be desperate to try to buy himself an Ego Prime.

So, all right, I was desperate. I'd spent eight years trying to keep Marge happy, which was exactly seven and a half years too long.

Marge was a dream to look at, with her tawny hair and her sulky eyes and a shape that could set your teeth chattering—but that was where the dream stopped.

She had a tongue like a #10 wood rasp and a list of grievances long enough to paper the bedroom wall. When she wasn't complaining, she was crying, and when she wasn't crying, she was pointing out in chilling detail exactly where George Faircloth fell short as a model husband, which happened to be everywhere. Half of the time she had a "beastly headache" (for which I was personally responsible) and the other half she was sore about something, so ninety-nine percent of the time we got along like a couple of tomcats in a packing case.

Maybe we just weren't meant for each other. I don't know. I used to envy guys like Harry Folsom at the office. His wife is no joy to live with either, but at least he could take a spin down to Rio once in a while with one of the stenographers and get away with it.

I knew better than to try. Marge was already so jealous that I couldn't even smile at the company receptionist without a twinge of guilt. Give Marge something real to howl about, and I'd be ready for the Rehab Center in a week.

But I'd underestimated Marge. She didn't need anything real, as I found out when Jeree came along.

Business was booming and the secretaries at the office got shuffled around from time to time. Since I had an executive-type job, I got an executive-type secretary. Her name was Jeree and she was gorgeous. As a matter of fact, she was better than gorgeous. She was the sort of secretary every businessman ought to have in his office. Not to do any work—just to sit there.

Jeree was tall and dark, and she could convey more without saying anything than I ever dreamed was possible. The first day she was there, she conveyed to me very clearly that if I cared to supply the opportunity, she'd be glad to supply the motive.

That night, I could tell that Marge had been thinking something over during the day. She let me get the first bite of dinner halfway to my mouth, and then she said, "I hear you got a new secretary today."

I muttered something into my coffee cup and pretended not to hear.

Marge turned on her Accusing Look #7. "I also hear that she's five-foot-eight and tapes out at 38-25-36 and thinks you're handsome."

Marge had quite a spy system.

"She couldn't be much of a secretary," she added.

"She's a perfectly good secretary," I blurted, and kicked myself mentally. I should have known Marge's traps by then.

Marge exploded. I didn't get any supper, and she was still going strong at midnight. I tried to argue, but when Marge got going, there was no stopping her. I had my ultimatum, as far as Jeree was concerned.

Harry Folsom administered the *coup de grace* at coffee next morning. "What you need is an Ego Prime," he said with a grin. "Solve all your problems. I hear they work like a charm."

I set my coffee cup down. Bells were ringing in my ears. "Don't be ridiculous. It's against the law. Anyway, I wouldn't think of such a thing. It's—it's indecent."

Harry shrugged. "Just joking, old man, just joking. Still, it's fun to think about, eh? Freedom from wife. Absolutely safe and harmless. Not even too expensive, if you've got the right contacts. And I've got a friend who knows a guy—"

Just then, Jeree walked past us and flashed me a big smile. I gripped my cup for dear life and still spilled coffee on my tie.

As I said, a guy gets fed up.

And maybe opportunity would only knock once.

And an Ego Prime would solve all my problems, as Harry had told me.

• • •

Vocabulary words:
Find these words in the section, write the sentence they are used in, and write your own definition. If you are stuck, look it up in the dictionary, but still write a definition in your own words.

grievances
ultimatum

Comprehension/extension questions:

What are some of the colorful expressions that you enjoyed from this passage? How do they set the tone for the story?

What do you think an Ego Prime is?

• • •

It was completely illegal, of course. The wonder was that Ego Prime, Inc., ever got to put their product on the market at all, once the nation's housewives got wind of just what their product was.

From the first, there was rigid Federal control and laws regulating the use of Primes right down to the local level. You could get a license for a Utility model Prime if you were a big business executive, or a high public official, or a movie star, or something like that; but even then his circuits had to be inspected every two months, and he had to have a thousand built-in Paralyzers, and you had to specify in advance exactly what you wanted your Prime to be able to do when, where, how, why, and under what circumstances.

The law didn't leave a man much leeway.

But everybody knew that if you *really* wanted a personal Prime with all his circuits open and no questions asked, you could get one. Black market prices were steep and you ran your own risk, but it could be done.

Harry Folsom told his friend who knew a guy, and a few greenbacks got lost somewhere, and I found myself looking at a greasy little man with a black mustache and a bald spot, up in a dingy fourth-story warehouse off lower Broadway.

"Ah, yes," the little man said. "Mr. Faircloth. We've been expecting you."

I didn't like the looks of the guy any more than the looks of the place. "I've been told you can supply me with a—"

He coughed. "Yes, yes. I understand. It might be possible." He fingered his mustache and regarded me from pouchy eyes. "Busy executives often come to us to avoid the—ah—unpleasantness of formal arrangements. Naturally, we only act as agents, you might say. We never see the merchandise ourselves—" He wiped his hands on his trousers. "Now were you interested in the ordinary Utility model, Mr. Faircloth?"

I assumed he was just being polite. You didn't come to the back door for Utility models.

"Or perhaps you'd require one of our Deluxe models. Very careful workmanship. Only a few key Paralyzers in operation and practically complete circuit duplication. Very useful for—ah—close contact work, you know. Social engagements, conferences—"

I was shaking my head. "I want a *Super* Deluxe model," I told him.

He grinned and winked. "Ah, indeed! You want perfect duplication. Yes, indeed. Domestic situations can be—awkward, shall we say. Very awkward—"

I gave him a cold stare. I couldn't see where my domestic problems were any affairs of his. He got the idea and hurried me back to a storeroom.

"We keep a few blanks here for the basic measurement. You'll go to our laboratory on 14th Street to have the minute impressions taken. But I can assure you you'll be delighted, simply delighted."

The blanks weren't very impressive—clay and putty and steel, faceless, brainless. He went over me like a tailor, checking measurements of all sorts. He was thorough—embarrassingly thorough, in fact—but finally he was finished. I went on to the laboratory.

And that was all there was to it.

Practical androids had been a pipe dream until Hunyadi invented the Neuro-pantograph. Hunyadi had no idea in the world what to do with it once he'd invented it, but a couple of enterprising engineers bought him body and soul, sub-contracted the problems of anatomy, design, artistry, audio and visio circuitry, and so forth, and ended up with the modern Ego Primes we have today.

I spent a busy two hours under the NP microprobes; the artists worked outside while the NP technicians worked inside. I came out of it pretty woozy, but a shot of Happy-O set that straight. Then I waited in the recovery room for another two hours, dreaming up ways to use my Prime when I got him. Finally the door opened and the head technician walked in, followed by a tall, sandy-haired man with worried blue eyes and a tired look on his face

"Meet George Faircloth Prime," the technician said, grinning at me like a nursing mother.

I shook hands with myself. Good firm handshake, I thought admiringly. Nothing flabby about it.

I slapped George Prime on the shoulder happily. "Come on, Brother," I said. "You've got a job to do."

But, secretly, I was wondering what Jeree was doing that night.

George Prime had remote controls, as well as a completely recorded neurological analogue of his boss, who was me. George Prime thought what I thought about the same things I did in the same way I did. The only difference was that what I told George Prime to do, George Prime did.

If I told him to go to a business conference in San Francisco and make the smallest possible concessions for the largest possible orders, he would go there and do precisely that. His signature would be my signature. It would hold up in court.

And if I told him that my wife Marge was really a sweet, goodhearted girl and that he was to stay home and keep her quiet and happy any time I chose, he'd do that, too.

George Prime was a duplicate of me right down to the sandy hairs on the back of my hands. Our fingerprints were the same. We had the same mannerisms and used the same figures of speech. The only physical difference apparent even to an expert was the tiny finger-depression buried in the hair above his ear. A little pressure there would stop George Prime dead in his tracks.

He was so lifelike, even I kept forgetting that he was basically just a pile of gears.

I'd planned very carefully how I meant to use him, of course.

Every man who's been married eight years has a sanctuary. He builds it up and maintains it against assault in the very teeth of his wife's natural instinct to clean, poke, pry and rearrange things. Sometimes it takes him years of diligent work to establish his hideout and be confident that it will stay inviolate, but if he starts early enough, and sticks with it long enough, and is fierce enough and persistent enough and crafty enough, he'll probably win in the end. The girls hate him for it, but he'll win.

With some men, it's just a box on their dressers, or a desk, or a corner of an unused back room. But I had set my sights high early in the game. With me, it was the whole workshop in the garage.

At first, Marge tried open warfare. She had to clean the place up, she said. I told her I didn't *want* her to clean it up. She could clean the whole house as often as she chose, but *I* would clean up the workshop.

After a couple of sharp engagements on that field, Marge staged a strategic withdrawal and reorganized her attack. A little pile of wood shavings would be on the workshop floor one night and be gone the next. A wrench would be back on the rack—upside down, of course. An open paint can would have a cover on it.

I always knew. I screamed loudly and bitterly. I ranted and raved. I swore I'd rig up a booby-trap with a shotgun.

So she quit trying to clean in there and just went in once in a while to take a look around. I fixed that with the old toothpick-in-the-door routine. Every time she so much as set foot in that workshop, she had a battle on her hands for the next week or so. She could count on it. It was that predictable.

She never found out how I knew, and after seven years or so, it wore her down. She didn't go into the workshop any more.

As I said, you've got to be persistent, but you'll win. Eventually.

If you're *really* persistent.

Now all my effort paid off. I got Marge out of the house for an hour or two that day and had George Prime delivered and stored in the big closet in the workshop. They hooked his controls up and left me a manual of instructions for running him. When I got home that night, there he was, just waiting to be put to work.

After supper, I went out to the workshop—to get the pipe I'd left there, I said. I pushed George Prime's button, winked at him and switched on the free-behavior circuits.

"Go to it, Brother," I said.

George Prime put my pipe in his mouth, lit it and walked back into the house.

Five minutes later, I heard them fighting.

It sounded so familiar that I laughed out loud. Then I caught a cab on the corner and headed uptown.

We had quite a night, Jeree and I. I got home just about time to start for work, and sure enough, there was George Prime starting my car, business suit on, briefcase under his arm.

I pushed the recall and George Prime got out of the car and walked into the workshop. He stepped into his cradle in the closet. I turned him off and then drove away in the car.

Bless his metallic soul, he'd even kissed Marge good-bye for me!

• • •

Vocabulary words:
Find these words in the section, write the sentence they are used in, and write your own definition. If you are stuck, look it up in the dictionary, but still write a definition in your own words.

concessions
mannerisms

Comprehension/extension questions:

What would you do with an android duplicate of yourself?

• • •

Needless to say, the affairs of George Faircloth took on a new sparkle with George Prime on hand to cover the home front.

For the first week, I was hardly home at all. I must say I felt a little guilty, leaving poor old George Prime to cope with Marge all the time—he looked and acted so human, it was easy to forget that he literally couldn't care less. But I felt apologetic all the same whenever I took him out of his closet.

"She's really a sweet girl underneath it all," I'd say. "You'll learn to like her after a bit."

123

"Of course I like her," George Prime said. "You told me to, didn't you? Stop worrying. She's really a sweet girl underneath it all."

He sounded convincing enough, but still it bothered me. "You're sure you understand the exchange mechanism?" I asked. I didn't want any foul-ups there, as you can imagine.

"Perfectly," said George Prime. "When you buzz the recall, I wait for the first logical opportunity I can find to come out to the workshop, and you take over."

"But you might get nervous. You might inadvertently tip her off."

George Prime looked pained. "Really, old man! I'm a Super Deluxe model, remember? I don't have fourteen activated Hunyadi tubes up in this cranial vault of mine just for nothing. You're the one that's nervous. I'll take care of everything. Relax."

So I did.

Jeree made good all her tacit promises and then some. She had a very cozy little apartment on 34th Street where we went to relax after a hard day at the office. When we weren't doing the town, that is. As long as Jeree didn't try too much conversation, everything was wonderful.

And then, when Jeree got a little boring, there was Sybil in the accounting department. Or Dorothy in promotion. Or Jane. Or Ingrid.

I could go on at some length, but I won't. I was building quite a reputation for myself around the office.

Of course, it was like buying your first 3-V[6] set. In a week or so, the novelty wears off a little and you start eating on schedule again. It took a little while, but I finally had things down to a reasonable program.

Tuesday and Thursday nights, I was informally "out" while formally "in." Sometimes I took Sunday nights "out" if things got too sticky around the house over the weekend. The rest of the time, George Prime cooled his heels in his closet. Locked up, of course. Can't completely trust a wife to observe a taboo, no matter how well trained she is.

There, was an irreconcilable amount of risk. George Prime had to quick-step some questions about my work at the office—there was no way to supply him with current data until the time for his regular two-month refill and pattern-accommodation at the laboratory. In the meantime, George Prime had to make do with what he had.

But as he himself pointed out he was a Super Deluxe model.

Marge didn't suspect a thing. In fact, George Prime seemed to be having a remarkable effect on her. I didn't notice anything at first—I was hardly ever home. But one night I found my pipe and slippers laid out for me, and the evening paper neatly folded on my chair, and it brought me up short. Marge had been extremely docile

---

[6] A pair of dice with less likelihood of throwing a 7 in craps.

lately. We hadn't had a good fight in days. Weeks, come to think of it.

I thought it over and shrugged. Old age, I figured. She was bound to mellow sometime.

But pretty soon I began to wonder if she wasn't mellowing a little too much.

One night when I got home, she kissed me almost as though she really meant it. There wasn't an unpleasant word all through dinner, which happened to be steak with mushrooms, served in the dining room (!) by candlelight (!!) with dinner music that Marge could never bear, chiefly because I liked it.

We sat over coffee and cigarettes, and it seemed almost like old times. *Very* old times, in fact I even caught myself looking at Marge again—really *looking* at her, watching the light catch in her hair, almost admiring the sparkle in her brown eyes. Sparkle, I said, not glint.

As I mentioned before, Marge was always easy to look at. That night, she was practically ravishing.

"What are you doing to her?" I asked George Prime later, out in the workshop.

"Why, nothing," said George Prime, looking innocent. He couldn't fool me with his look, though, because it was exactly the look I use when I'm guilty and pretending to be innocent.

"There must be *something*."

George Prime shrugged. "Any woman will warm up if you spend enough time telling her all the things she wants to hear and pay all the attention to her that she wants paid to her. That's elemental psychology. I can give you page references."

I ought to mention that George Prime had a complete set of basic texts run into his circuits, at a slightly additional charge. Never can tell when an odd bit of information will come in useful.

"Well, you must be doing quite a job," I said. *I'd* never managed to warm Marge up much.

"I try," said George Prime.

"Oh, I'm not complaining," I hastened to add, forgetting that a Prime's feelings can't be hurt and that he was only acting like me because it was in character. "I was just curious."

"Of course, George."

"I'm really delighted that you're doing so well."

"Thank you, George."

But the next night when I was with Dawn, who happens to be a gorgeous redhead who could put Marge to shame on practically any field of battle except maybe brains, I kept thinking about Marge all evening long, and wondering if things weren't getting just a little out of hand.

• • •

Vocabulary words:
Find these words in the section, write the sentence they are used in, and write your own definition. If you are stuck, look it up in the dictionary, but still write a definition in your own words.

inadvertently
tacit
irreconcilable

Comprehension/extension questions:

Why is George concerned about his relationship with Marge?

• • •

The next evening I almost tripped over George Prime coming out of a liquor store. I ducked quickly into an alley and flagged him. "What are you doing out on the street?"

He gave me my martyred look. "Just buying some bourbon. You were out."

"But you're not supposed to be off the premises—"

"Marge asked me to come. I couldn't tell her I was sorry, but her husband wouldn't let me, could I?"

"Well, certainly not—"

"You want me to keep her happy, don't you? You don't want her to get suspicious."

"No, but suppose somebody saw us together! If she ever got a hint—"

"I'm sorry," George Prime said contritely. "It seemed the right thing to do. You would have done it. At least that's what my judgment center maintained. We had quite an argument."

"Well, tell your judgment center to use a little sense," I snapped. "I don't want it to happen again."

The next night, I stayed home, even though it was Tuesday night. I was beginning to get worried. Of course, I did have complete control—I could snap George Prime off any time I wanted, or even take him in for a complete recircuiting—but it seemed a pity. He was doing such a nice job.

Marge was docile as a kitten, even more so than before. She sympathized with my hard day at the office and agreed heartily that the boss, despite all appearances, was in reality a jabbering idiot. After dinner, I suggested a movie, but Marge gave me an odd sort of look and said she thought it would be much nicer to spend the evening at home by the fire.

I'd just gotten settled with the paper when she came into the living room and sat down beside me. She was wearing some sort of filmy affair I'd never laid eyes on before, and I caught a whiff of my favorite perfume.

"Georgie?" she said.

"Uh?"

"Do you still love me?"

I set the paper down and stared at her. "How's that? Of course I still—"

"Well, sometimes you don't act much like it."

"Mm. I guess I've—uh—got an awful headache tonight." Damn that perfume!

"Oh," said Marge.

"In fact, I thought I'd turn in early and get some sleep—"

"Sleep," said Marge. There was no mistaking the disappointment in her voice. Now I knew that things were out of hand.

The next evening, I activated George Prime and caught the taxi at the corner, but I called Ruby and broke my date with her. I took in an early movie alone and was back by ten o'clock. I left the cab at the corner and walked quietly up the path toward the garage.

Then I stopped. I could see Marge and George Prime through the living room windows.

George Prime was kissing my wife the way I hadn't kissed her in eight long years. It made my hair stand on end. And Marge wasn't exactly fighting him off, either. She was coming back for more. After a little, the lights went off.

George Prime was a Super Deluxe model, all right.

I dashed into the workshop and punched the recall button as hard as I could, swearing under my breath. How long had this been going on? I punched the button again, viciously, and waited.

George Prime didn't come out.

It was plenty cold out in the workshop that night and I didn't sleep a wink. About dawn, out came George Prime, looking like a man with a four-day hangover.

Our conversation got down to fundamentals. George Prime kept insisting blandly that, according to my own directions, he was to pick the first logical opportunity to come out when I buzzed, and that was exactly what he'd done.

I was furious all the way to work. I'd take care of this nonsense, all right. I'd have George Prime rewired from top to bottom as soon as the laboratory could take him.

But I never phoned the laboratory. The bank was calling me when I got to the office. They wanted to know what I planned to do about that check of mine that had just bounced.

"What check?" I asked.

"The one you wrote to cash yesterday—five hundred dollars—against your regular account, Mr. Faircloth."

The last I'd looked, I'd had about three thousand dollars in that account. I told the man so rather bluntly.

"Oh, no, sir. That is, you *did* until last week. But all these checks you've been cashing have emptied the account."

He flashed the checks on the desk screen. My signature was on every one of them.

"What about my special account?" I'd learned long before that an account Marge didn't know about was sound rear-guard strategy.

"That's been closed out for two weeks."

I hadn't written a check against that account for over a year! I glared at the ceiling and tried to think things through.

I came up with a horrible thought.

Marge had always had her heart set on a trip to Bermuda. Just to get away from it all, she'd say. A second honeymoon.

I got a list of travel agencies from the business directory and started down them. The third one I tried had a pleasant tenor voice. "No, sir, not *Mrs.* Faircloth. *You* bought two tickets. One way. Champagne flight to Bermuda."

"When?" I choked out.

"Why, today, as a matter of fact. It leaves Idlewild at eleven o'clock—"

I let him worry about my amnesia and started home fast. I didn't know what they'd given that Prime for circuits, but there was no question now that he was out of control—*way* out of control. And poor Marge, all worked up for a second honeymoon—

Then it struck me. Poor Marge? Poor sucker George! No Prime in his right circuits would behave this way without some human guidance and that meant only one thing: Marge had spotted him. It had happened before. Couple of nasty court battles I'd read about. And she'd known all about George Prime.

For how long?

• • •

Vocabulary words:
Find these words in the section, write the sentence they are used in, and write your own definition. If you are stuck, look it up in the dictionary, but still write a definition in your own words.

martyred
contritely
fundamentals

Comprehension/extension questions:

What has gone wrong? Why isn't George having the fun that he expected to?

• • •

When I got home, the house was empty. George Prime wasn't in his closet. And Marge wasn't in the house.

They were gone.

I started to call the police, but caught myself just in time. I couldn't very well complain to the cops that my wife had run off with an android.

Worse yet, I could get twenty years for having an illegal Prime wandering around.

I sat down and poured myself a stiff drink.

My own wife deserting me for a pile of bearings.

It was indecent.

Then I heard the front door open and there was Marge, her arms full of grocery bundles. "Why, darling! You're home early!"

I just blinked for a moment. Then I said, "You're still here!"

"Of course. Where did you think I'd be?"

"But I thought—I mean the ticket office—"

She set down the bundles and kissed me and looked up into my eyes, almost smiling, half reproachful. "You didn't really think I'd go running off with something out of a lab, did you?"

"Then—you knew?"

"Certainly I knew, silly. You didn't do a very good job of instructing him, either. You gave him far too much latitude. Let him have ideas of his own and all that. And next thing I knew, he was trying to get me to run off with him to Hawaii or someplace."

"Bermuda," I said.

And then Marge was in my arms, kissing me and snuggling her cheek against my chest.

"Even though he looked like you, I knew he couldn't be," she said. "He was like you, but he wasn't *you*, darling. And all I ever want is you. I just never appreciated you before…."

I held her close and tried to keep my hands from shaking. George Faircloth, Idiot, I thought. She'd never been more beautiful. "But what did you do with him?"

"I sent him back to the factory, naturally. They said they could blot him out and use him over again. But let's not talk about that any more. We've got more interesting things to discuss."

Maybe we had, but we didn't waste a lot of time talking. It was the Marge I'd once known and I was beginning to wonder how I could have been so wrong about her. In fact unless my memory was getting awfully porous, the old Marge was *never* like this—

I kissed her tenderly and ran my hands through her hair, and felt the depression with my forefinger, and then I knew what had really happened.

That Marge always had been a sly one.

I wondered how she was liking things in Bermuda.

Marge probably thought she'd really put me where I belonged, but the laugh was on her, after all.

As I said, the old Marge was never like the new one. Marge Prime makes Jeree and Sybil and Dorothy and Dawn and Jane and Ruby all look pretty sad by comparison.

She cooks like a dream and she always brings me my pipe and slippers. As they say, there's nothing a man likes more than to be appreciated.

A hundred percent appreciated, with a factory guarantee to correct any slippage, which would only be temporary, anyhow.

One of these days, we'll take that second honeymoon. But I think we'll go to Hawaii.

• • •

Vocabulary words:
Find these words in the section, write the sentence they are used in, and write your own definition. If you are stuck, look it up in the dictionary, but still write a definition in your own words.

slippage

Comprehension/extension questions:

Who got the last laugh?

Did things turn out the way that George had expected? Better? Worse?

What would you do with an android? How would it change your life?

Prime Difference, by Alan E. Nourse, Published June 1957

Alan E. Nourse was born in Des Moines, Iowa on August 11, 1918 and died July 19, 1992. He was the prolific author of novels, short stories, and essays from the 1950s to 1980s. He also wrote under the names Doctor X.

THE PILOT AND THE BUSHMAN

By SYLVIA JACOBS
Illustrated by DAVID STONE

**Technological upheavals caused by inventions of
our own are bad enough, but this was the ultimate
depression, caused by
the ultimate alien invention—which no Earthman
ever saw!**

The Ambassador from Outer Space sprang to his feet, taking Jerry's extended hand in a firm, warm grasp. Jerry had been prepared for almost anything—a scholarly brontosaurus, perhaps, or an educated squid or giant caterpillar with telepathic powers. But the Ambassador didn't even have antennae, gills, or green hair. He was a completely normal and even handsome human being.

"Scotch? Cigar?" the Ambassador offered cordially. "How can I help you, Mr. Jergins?"

Studying him, Jerry decided there *was* something peculiar about this extraterrestrial, after all. He was too perfect. His shave was too close, his skin so unblemished as to suggest wax-works. Every strand of his distinguished iron-gray hair was impeccably placed. The negligent and just-right drape of his clothes covered a body shaped like a Sixth Century B.C. piece of Greek sculpture. No mere human could have looked so unruffled, so utterly groomed, at three o'clock in the afternoon, in a busy office. A race, Jerry wondered, capable of taking any shape at will, in mimicry of the indigenous race of any planet?

"You *can* help me, but I'm not sure you *will*," Jerry said. "The rumor is that you won't do anything to ease this buyers' strike you started on Earth."

The Ambassador smiled. "You're a man who's not used to taking no for an answer, I gather. What's your proposition?"

"I'd like to contact some of the firms on the Federated Planets, show them how I could promote their merchandise on Earth. Earth is already clamoring for their goods. To establish a medium of exchange, we'd have to run simultaneous campaigns, promoting Earth merchandise on other planets."

"That would be difficult, even for a man of your promotional ability," the Ambassador said winningly. "You see, Earth is the only planet we've yet discovered where advertising—or promotion, to use the broader term—exists as a social and economic force."

"How in hell can anybody do business without it?" Jerry demanded.

"We don't do business in the sense you mean. Don't mistake me," the Ambassador added hastily, "we don't have precisely a communal economy, either. Our very well defined sense of ethics in regard to material goods is something I find impossible to describe in any Earth language. It's quite simple, so simple that you have to grow up with it to understand it. Our whole attitude toward material goods is conditioned by the Matter Repositor."

"*That* gadget!" Jerry said bitterly. "It was when you first mentioned it before the U.N. Assembly that all this trouble on Earth started. Everybody and his brother hopes that tomorrow he can buy a Matter Repositor, and never have to buy anything again. I came here mostly to ask you whether it's really true, that if you have one of those dinguses, you can bring anything you want into your living room."

"You *can*. In practice, of course, repositing just anything that took your fancy would produce economic anarchy."

"Let's put it this way," Jerry persisted. "Home appliances were my biggest accounts. Now, when we try to sell a refrigerator, the prospect says she's saving her cash till Matter Repositors get on the Earth market. She plans to reposit a refrigerator—not from her neighbor's kitchen, because that would be stealing—but from the factory. If the factory goes bust, people figure the government will have to subsidize building appliances. Now, could she really reposit a refrigerator?"

"She could. But she wouldn't want to."

"Why not?" Jerry asked, puzzled.

"If she conceived an illogical and useless desire for food refrigeration, she would simply reposit a block of cold air from, say, the North Pole."

"Oh, fine!" Jerry said sarcastically. "That would cause more unemployment in the refrigerator industry than repositing them without paying for them! But what do you mean about food refrigeration being illogical and useless?"

"Well, in a storage warehouse, there might be some reason for food preservation. But you don't need cold or canning. Why not just reposit the bacteria that cause the food to deteriorate? There's no need to store food in a home equipped with a Matter Repositor. You simply reposit one meal at a time. Fruits and vegetables direct from tree or field. Meat from a slaughterhouse, since it isn't humane to remove a pound of steak from a live steer. But even this is needless."

"Why?" Jerry baffledly wanted to know.

"To free the maximum amount of the effort of thinking beings for non-material activities, each consumer can reposit the chemical elements of the food, synthesize his meal on the table. He can even reposit these elements directly into his stomach, or, to bypass the effort of digestion, into his bloodstream as glycogen and amino acids."

"So refrigerators would be as dead an item as kerosene lamps in a city wired for electricity," Jerry agreed unhappily. "Suppose Mrs. Housewife, not needing a refrigerator, reposits a washing machine. The point I'm driving at—is there any practical way to compensate the factory, give it an incentive to produce more washing machines, without dragging in government control?"

"Why should the factory produce more washing machines? Who would want one? The housewife would simply reposit the dirt from her clothes into her flowerbed, without using water and soap. Or, more likely, reposit new clothes with different colors, fabrics, and styles. The Matter Repositor would eliminate textile mills and clothing factories. Earth's oceans have vast enough quantities of seaweed to eliminate the growing of cotton, wool, or flax. Or, again, you could reposit the chemical elements, either from the soil or from seawater."

Jerry pondered the extensive implications of these revelations. Finally he said, "What it boils down to is this. All Earth's bustling material activity, all the logging and construction, the mining and manufacturing, the planting and fishing, the printing and postal service, the great transportation and shipping effort, the cleaning and painting, the sewage disposal, even the bathing and self-adornment, consist, when you analyze them, of one process only—*putting something from where you don't want it to where you do*. There's not one single, solitary Earth invention or service left to advertise!"

"Nothing," the Ambassador agreed. "Which is exactly why advertising has not developed on the Federated Planets. You're fortunate that Earth doesn't have Matter Repositors. You'd be out of a job if it did."

"Oh, no!" Jerry said. "I could still advertise the gadget to end all gadgets—the Matter Repositor itself. I know other people have asked you this before, but could an Earth company get a franchise to import those machines here, or the license rights to manufacture them?"

"No," the Ambassador said, briefly and definitely.

"Mr. Ambassador," Jerry protested, "you've gone to a lot of trouble to explain things you must already be tired of explaining to Earthmen, just so I personally could be sure they weren't merely rumors or misinterpretations. Now that I get down to the real point, you suddenly become blunt and unqualified. Why?"

"Because there's a very serious question of ethics involved, wherever a more advanced civilization comes in contact with a relatively primitive one. For instance, when the white men came to America, the aborigines were introduced to gunpowder and firewater."

"So you people are keeping Matter Repositors away from us, like a mama keeping candy away from a baby who's hollering for it, because it's not good for him! You'd pass up a chance to name your own price—"

"The very way you phrase that remark indicates the danger. You regard personal gain as the strongest of motives, which means that Matter Repositors would be used for that, even by such unusually intelligent members of your race as yourself."

"Don't softsoap me," Jerry said angrily. "Not after you just got through saying that we Earthlings are nothing but naked savages, compared to the high and mighty super-beings on other planets!"

"I apologize for my phraseology," the Ambassador said. "With my limited command of your language—"

"Your limited command, nuts! I suppose you supermen enjoy seeing us naked savages squirm. Why talk sanctimoniously about the damage you might do, when you know damn well the damage has already been done? Just the news that something as advanced as the Matter Repositor exists has sent unemployment to a new high, and the stock market to a new low. And you theorize about ethics, while denying us the only cure!" Jerry found himself fighting a nearly irresistible impulse to smash his fist into that too-perfect profile—which, he realized glumly, would only prove the Ambassador's point about savages.

"Here, here," the Ambassador said benevolently, "let's have another drink. Then we'll see whether I can make it clear to you why the actual importation of Matter Repositors would cause much more trouble on Earth than the announcement of their existence, bad as the effect of that has been. To begin with, I admit I made a very serious error in mentioning the device at all before the U.N. Assembly. I intended merely to explain how I came here without a spaceship. After that, I was flooded with questions; I could no more avoid answering them than I could courteously avoid answering the questions you've been asking today."

"You mean you super-beings actually admit you're human enough to make mistakes?" Jerry asked, somewhat mollified.

"Of course we make mistakes. We try not to make the same one twice. You see, we once made the mistake of importing Matter Repositors to a planet whose natural resources and social concepts weren't adequate for the device. That was a long time ago, and they haven't recovered from the effects yet. Suppose a consignment of ten thousand Matter Repositors arrived on Earth tomorrow. Under your economic system, who would get them?"

"The ten thousand people or corporations who had the most money to pay for them, I guess. Unless government agencies grabbed 'em."

"Can you guarantee that of the ten thousand people on Earth who have the most money, not one is unscrupulous?"

"Gosh, no!" Jerry said. "I don't think there's any doubt that to stay in business very long, a man or a company has to have a certain amount of business ethics. Nobody can gyp the public indefinitely. But a bank robber might have a lot of cash, or a confidence man, or a cluck with a big inheritance."

"So, to be generous, let's assume that 9,999 of your wealthiest persons are so ethical that they would never make any profit at the expense of the general welfare. That leaves us one crook. What would he reposit first?"

"Hmm.... Maybe the gold at Fort Knox."

"And what effect would that have on Earth's business?"

"I'm not quite sure," Jerry admitted. "I'm no shark on monetary theory, just the kind of large-scale salesman who makes mass production possible. But it certainly wouldn't do the world situation any good."

"Suppose, next, our crook holds the President of the United States for ransom. Since he doesn't need money, the ransom price might be laws which would grant him impunity for his crimes. If not, he could have an accomplice reposit him out of jail, or even out of the electric chair, before the switch was pulled."

"That's enough! I get the idea!" Jerry exclaimed.

"Wait—there's a more important point. Suppose a government you consider the wrong government got hold of some of the machines. First, of course, they'd reposit the world stockpile of atomic bombs. Then they'd reposit disease bacteria into the bloodstreams of U.N. troops, officials, and civilian workers, and reposit all the ammunition out of U.N. guns. So long as there is one spark of nationalism left on Earth, so long as any country has an economic and political system they consider better than some other system, Matter Repositors would mean planetary self-destruction. Now do you see why I was blunt and unqualified?"

"I do," Jerry said solemnly, "And I was a fool to fly off the handle when you called us savages. We are savages, I can see that now. And your people must be pretty damned godlike to be trusted with such an invention!"

"Not at all. To a Micronesian bushman, the pilot who can be trusted with the power and speed of a B-29 seems a veritable god. But the pilot is only an ordinary Joe, very likely no more intelligent than the bushman— he just had a different background. Fighting each other for necessities and luxuries, the process that you people call business competition, has so long been needless to our people that they would no more think of competitive gain than you would do an Indian harvest dance before you signed a contract. They aren't necessarily more intelligent or more virtuous than your people—they just have a different background."

"You seem to have devoted a lot of study to the larceny in the Earthman's soul," Jerry put in. "What if we stole the secret from you, whether you think it wise to give it to us or not? Suppose somebody swiped the blueprints, or copied a Repositor you brought with you for your own use?"

The Ambassador smiled. "You might *try* to steal it. That's why I didn't bring a Repositor with me, to save you people the trouble of a futile try."

"Why futile?"

"Well, the Matter Repositor is a simple device. Any child on the Federated Planets who had an education, say, equivalent to your technical high school education, could build a working model, even without another Repositor to assist him. But Earth's best technicians couldn't build one, even with either blueprints or a model to copy."

"They couldn't, eh?" Jerry challenged, bristling again. "They managed to split atoms, transmute elements, do a few little tricks like that."

"I see I've been tactless again," the Ambassador said regretfully. "Just now, you readily conceded that Earthmen are savages morally, but when I seem to cast aspersions on your mechanical ability, it offends your racial vanity. All right, let's go back to the B-29 pilot and the intelligent bushman. The internal combustion engine that powers the B-29 is a simple device in fundamental principle, isn't it?"

"Sure," Jerry said.

"Any high school boy who has taken a course in auto mechanics, who has the requisite machine tools, metals, casting equipment, and fuel, could build a working model of an internal combustion engine, couldn't he, even without ready-made parts?"

"If he wasn't all thumbs, he could."

"All right. Now suppose the B-29 is grounded in the jungle. The bushman is examining the engine. He's just as intelligent as the pilot, remember, but his environment hasn't produced an oil well, let alone a refinery. He has never seen a lathe or a micrometer. He has no mine, no smelter. He can't copy that B-29 engine by whittling wood or chipping stone, even if he's a born mechanical genius, and he can't run it on seawater. So he says the plane flies by magic. Put him in the pilot seat, and you'll admit it's practically inevitable that he'll crash."

"Why do you take so much trouble to explain things?" Jerry asked wryly. "I should have my head examined for not understanding it in the first place."

"Let's say I'm feebly trying to make amends for what my unfortunate slip of the tongue has done to your business."

"You've brought me around to your way of thinking, Mr. Ambassador," Jerry said, recovering enough to carry the ball. "But it would be impossible to sell the public on the idea that they shouldn't have Repositors because they're too hot to handle. Statistics on auto accidents never convinced anybody that he didn't want a nice, shiny, new car. Nobody thinks he personally will get killed in traffic—he's too smart. You can't convince a youngster he doesn't want candy before dinner; he thinks he knows better than his parents. But you can hide the candy, while putting an appetizing meal on the table."

"Yes, except that I regrettably didn't hide the fact that the Matter Repositor exists."

"You sure didn't. And it puts you on a spot, doesn't it? I don't imagine it will be much fun for you to report to your government that one ill-considered remark, made shortly after your arrival, upset Earth's economy."

For the first time, the Ambassador's suavity was ruffled. Sweat stood out on his noble forehead. "I've been hoping the bad effects would die down before I have to report," he confessed.

"They won't die down by themselves. You know damned well they're getting worse and worse, as word-of-mouth advertising about the Matter Repositor spreads." Jerry leaned closer. "But you and I can get rid of those bad effects."

"How?"

"Well, I'll tell you. When I came to see you, I was pretty sure you'd turn me down cold on importing Matter Repositors. But I had an ace up my sleeve. I hoped you would admit that the reason you've been stalling on selling Earth any Repositors is that you don't really have a practical one. I thought maybe rumors of the Repositor's powers had been vastly exaggerated. If you admitted that, I intended to publicize it to the limit.

A campaign to convince Earthmen that you'd been kidding them would work, because it plays on John Q. Public's conviction that he's pretty smart, too smart to believe all this gab about a gadget he's never seen. With your denial to back me up, I could put it across. It would be a lifesaving shot in the arm for Earth business."

"You mean," the Ambassador said reflectively, "that if I call myself a liar—if I actually become a liar in so doing—I can patch up the damage I've done? That puts me in a difficult ethical position."

"Not as difficult as the one you're in now. If it will make it easier for you, I can word your denial in a face-saving way, and have it ready for your signature Tuesday. You have a remarkable command of colloquial English, but even a diplomat using his native tongue can't juggle the connotations and inferences like an advertising man."

"It's very kind of you to offer your professional skill in my behalf. I think I should pay you a fee for the copy."

"Skip it," Jerry said generously, fingering the nickel and two pennies in his pocket. "A small token of my appreciation for the patience you've shown. What time Tuesday?"

"Say two o'clock?"

"Fine. But before I spend my time on this, you're not going to make the same deal with somebody else, are you?"

"Deal? Did I make a deal?"

"What I mean, nobody else has approached you with the idea that Earth business would get back to normal if you would deny that a practical Matter Repositor exists? You'd say I have exclusive rights to the idea?"

"Nobody has," the Ambassador said, "and I agree to give you exclusive rights."

"Good! With your signed denial, I can raise the loot. I think the N.A.M. will go for it. The campaign will have to be well-financed, you see; the amount of space the news columns will give to your denial may be as much as they gave to your original statement, but that alone won't do the job. It's much harder to kill a notion that has penetrated the public mind than it is to implant one."

• • •

Vocabulary words:
Find these words in the section, write the sentence they are used in, and write your own definition. If you are stuck, look it up in the dictionary, but still write a definition in your own words.

cordially
indigenous
softsoap
sanctimoniously
colloquial

Comprehension/extension questions:

What would you do first with a matter repositor?

How would a matter repositor affect your job/your parents' jobs?

What would be the effect of one person or one nation having everything they wanted?

• • •

The Ambassador indulged in a chuckle. "I'm beginning to see daylight. My signed denial in your hands becomes a salable piece of merchandise, worth far more than I would pay you for a few lines of copy. Well, more power to you! Would it be out of place for me to contribute some of the funds for publicizing this denial?"

"How much?" Jerry asked practically.

"Well," the Ambassador explained, "I've had nothing reposited that I could avoid. But since your planet has a monetary exchange, I had to pay for my office help, lodging, and so on. Synthesizing coinage would have been counterfeiting, which is against your laws, so I merely had a moderate amount of uncoined gold reposited, and I sell it on the regular Earth market as I need funds. Gold has no particular value on the Federated Planets, of course. I could get whatever you need, so long as it isn't enough to disrupt the economy any more than—well, than I have already. Let's limit ourselves to an amount that could be accounted for by an unusually good year in mining."

"Sold!" Jerry said happily. "I think I can struggle along on a million a month retainer. Plus the usual

151

fifteen percent on advertising space and printing, of course; I'll have an estimate on that for you Tuesday. Since you can finance the whole campaign yourself, we'll leave the N.A.M. out of it. That way I can spare you the humiliation of signing an outright denial. All you have to do from now on is to keep mum. Don't even admit that you're the angel financing this campaign; that would make it look phony. I'll assign you three personal public-relations men, on twenty-four-hour shift. All your public remarks are to screen through them."

"But how can I conceal my identity when I'm sponsoring the campaign?" the Ambassador objected.

"That's easy. The ostensible sponsor will be a dummy organization called—um—the Consumers Fact Finding Board. Nobody but me needs to know who signs the checks."

"How long will this campaign continue?"

"I figure it'll take about six months to sell the public this particular bill of goods. Once we get business revived, the best thing is never to mention the words Matter Repositor again, not even to deny its existence. The ultimate goal is to make people forget they ever heard of such a gadget. The more convincing I make it, the quicker I'll work myself out of a job."

"I should think you'd make it last as long as possible; that's why I asked you for a time-limit. Do you *want* to work yourself out of a job?"

"You bet I do! Then I can start selling a bigger item, launch a longer-term promotion, one that will last till Earth gets civilized, till I don't have anything more to sell. From what you say, that will take a lot longer than I'll live."

"It may be none of my business, but what is this big item you propose to sell next?" the Ambassador asked, curiously.

"Earth," Jerry said.

The Ambassador looked confused. "I'm afraid I don't understand."

"Didn't you just get through telling me, in effect, that any of your people who came to Earth could have all the money they wanted to spend? Well, I'm going to run advertising copy on the Federated Planets, and get them to come here and spend it."

"But I also told you that advertising is unknown on the Federated Planets!" the Ambassador protested.

"All the better. Your people, then, will have less sales resistance than an audience of Earth kindergarten kids, who have had spot commercials dinned into their ears since birth. The only problem is space and time."

"The Matter Repositor has effectively solved the problems of space and time."

"No, I mean space and time as an advertising man uses those terms. Newspaper and magazine space, radio and TV time. Do you have any newspapers out there?"

"We have very little you would classify as news. No wars, no stock market, no crime, no epidemics, no political mudslinging, few accidents. But we do have information bulletins, of course."

"Fine! Besides that million a month retainer, I want an exclusive contract to run advertising copy in the information bulletins on the Federated Planets."

"This is completely unprecedented!"

"You want to get out of this mess you're in, don't you? I'm the boy who can get you out, and that's my price."

"You drive a hard bargain, Mr. Jergins. Very well, I'll arrange it. But I'm getting you the contract only because I'm certain your excursion idea won't work. Oh, I know Earth men want to visit the Federated Planets; I've had plenty of requests. I've had to explain repeatedly that we must hold to our announced policy of no ambassador from Earth, and no exchange students, until Earth has completed a few more steps in the development of her civilization. But surely none of our people will come to Earth, aside from a few students of comparative civilizations. Our general public can view samples of your national costumes, automobiles, and so on, in the museums. I can't see why they should want to come here, while Earth is still in a primitive and dangerous stage."

"You can't, eh? Well, you might be surprised, Mr. Ambassador, you might be surprised. For the time being, just picture yourself as the pilot of that B-29, grounded on a primitive little island in space. You've met a poor, ignorant bushman. He couldn't reproduce your plane to save his neck. He can't manufacture a single gadget you'd want to buy. Nevertheless, you're about to see a demonstration of a few tricks of survival that your super-civilized race has forgotten—or, rather, never knew. I think you'll cook up into a right tasty dish."

• • •

Vocabulary words:
Find these words in the section, write the sentence they are used in, and write your own definition. If you are stuck, look it up in the dictionary, but still write a definition in your own words.

angel
ostensible

Comprehension/extension questions:

What do you think of Jergins' plan? Do you think the aliens will be interested in coming to see the earth?

How would extraterrestrials who are unused to advertising copy react to the commercials Jergins plans to run?

• • •

Four days later, the Better Business Bureau of Oskaloosa, Iowa, nabbed a questionable character who had accepted deposits from local businessmen, in return for elaborately printed but worthless contracts to deliver Matter Repositors.

The warning flash crossed similar warnings from New Orleans, Reno, Milwaukee, and the Borough of Queens, with a particularly hysterical note injected by Los Angeles, where the populace had proved most susceptible to the bogus agents. The news of a national ring of confidence artists, capitalizing on people's desire for Matter Repositors, ran in all papers, of course. The editors as yet hadn't the faintest idea that they were printing carefully engineered publicity.

Before he even got his space contracts lined up, Jerry had accomplished quite a feat. He had fixed things so that, if the Ambassador from Outer Space himself had changed his mind, and imported a cargo of genuine Matter Repositors, he would have had some trouble convincing people he wasn't a crook.

In a record two weeks, the campaign proper was ready to roll. It was long on white space, and the copy was so short that, after glancing at it a few times, you found that you had involuntarily committed it to memory. In the center of blank pages in all major metropolitan newspapers appeared a small want-ad, stating that the Consumers Fact Finding Board had deposited with a New York bank the sum of one million dollars in cash, *after taxes*, which would be paid to any person, terrestrial or extraterrestrial, who could produce a Matter Repositor capable of repositing an object weighing two pounds a distance of ten feet.

The offer was repeated daily for a month, and from the second day forward, there was a large, red overprint, looking like a crayon scrawl, which said, "No Takers to Date who Can Deliver the Goods!"

The idea was pounded into the public mind by car cards, billboards, direct mail, and annoying telephone solicitors, who got subscribers out of bathtub and bed to ask them whether they had a Matter Repositor around the house they wanted to sell for a million dollars. Skywriters by day and illuminated blimps by night made sure the literate could not escape the message. Radio and TV singing and cartoon commercials took care of the illiterate.

No conclusions were drawn in the copy. Each "prospect" was left with the comfortable feeling that his own superior intellect and powers of deduction had supplied the answer. No Matter Repositor turned up for sale, so everyone was sure there was no such thing. The whole campaign, like other advertising campaigns before it, depended on what people failed to consider. They neglected to realize that a million dollars would be a joke to the owner of a Matter Repositor, who could reposit all the wealth on Earth, including the million in the New York bank, but would have no use for money, since he could reposit usable goods. The magic phrase "a million dollars" was a worldwide symbol for all desirable material things. It would have been almost heresy to reflect that even that much cash had no actual value.

As Jerry promised, the Ambassador didn't have to issue an official denial. His chief public relations man quite truthfully admitted to reporters that the Ambassador had no Matter Repositor in his possession, a dispatch carried by all wire services, and snickered at by clever columnists.

In basements and garages, persons of good, bad, and indifferent mechanical ability strove to earn the million. The U.S. patent office was inundated with models and drawings of unworkable devices. One of the Duke University subjects tried to patent his ability to influence the fall of dice mentally.

During the next session of the Congress, Jerry's crack lobbyists raised a great howl about the shameful congestion in the Patent Office, not mentioning, of course, that they were employed by the man who had created the congestion, by offering a million dollars for a device he knew no Earthman could build.

Another dummy organization, dubbed the Inventors Protective League, sponsored a bill to amend the act relating to perpetual motion machines. It passed, with an emergency clause, and, thereafter, devices purporting to reposit matter were not entitled to letters of patent.

This just about clinched the deal, for the vast majority of people, who had never watched laws enacted, assumed that if something was in the law, there must be a good reason for it, unless, of course, it was anything like prohibition.

A name band revived "The Thing," leaving the drumbeats out of the vocal refrain, and substituting, "Get out of here with that Matter Repositor, before I call a cop!" Within six months, radio and TV comedians had worn out the joke. Even Goofy, My Friend Irma, Mrs. Ace, and Gracie Allen were too sophisticated to believe in Matter Repositors. Gags about them dropped to the same low level as those about Brooklyn and joke-stealing comics.

Although his appearance in public was liable to start boos and catcalls, the Ambassador from Outer Space was duly grateful. He was spared the painful necessity of reporting his disastrous slip of the tongue to his government, for Earth economy was again on the upward spiral. Everybody was spending the money he'd been saving up for a Matter Repositor.

The Ambassador cheerfully paid the million-a-month retainer and the whopping space bills, but Jerry's greatest gain in the transaction was his agreement allowing him to run advertising in the Federated Planets information bulletins. The space didn't cost him a nickel. Yet he knew how to sell his exclusive rights to it for more money than any one Earth company had in its promotional budget.

By the time the campaign debunking the Matter Repositor was ready to die a natural death, Jerry had started an organization of Earth businessmen, spearheaded by the Restaurant and Hotel Associations, and the transportation interests, to promote Earth as a primitive planet. The primitive aspects of Earth, Jerry predicted, would exert a powerful appeal on the citizens of the Federated Planets, who must be pretty bored with civilization, and badly in need of a vacation from too much perfection.

This organization was not composed of dummies, by any means, but the businessmen joined up with a vague idea that their hostelries were to be way-stations, that they were going to promote sightseeing tours to places they themselves would call primitive, that the human exhibits would consist of blanketed Navajos, Chinese coolies,[7] hula girls, Voodoo dancers, and Eskimos.

---

[7] Indentured servants

Jerry filled the biggest convention hall in Chicago, and, at the climax of the proceedings, dramatically drew back a velvet curtain, unveiling a huge painting of the symbol of the campaign—a masked bandit, wearing a slouch hat, clutching in a greedy hand a fat bag marked with a dollar sign. Below was blazoned the tasteful slogan, "Let the People of Earth Gyp You!"

• • •

Vocabulary words:
Find these words in the section, write the sentence they are used in, and write your own definition. If you are stuck, look it up in the dictionary, but still write a definition in your own words.

literate
heresy
hostelries

Comprehension/extension questions:

How did Jerry convince the people of earth that there were no Matter Repositors?

What earth experience was he trying to sell to extra-terrestrials?

• • •

A chorus of outrage echoed in the rafters. It hadn't occurred to the members that primitive exhibit A would be themselves; to wit, the genus Earth businessman; sub-species, go-getter. Jerry emerged from the resulting argument somewhat battered, but with what any experienced advertising man would recognize as a victory. His copy was to run in five percent of the space, keyed. Now all he had to do was prove in dollars and cents that he knew more about mass sales psychology than his clients, which was, of course, a cinch.

In spite of translation into a more civilized language, Jerry's five percent of the space out-pulled the tamer ninety-five percent by better than ten to one. Thereafter, his clients swallowed their pride, voted him a free hand, and contented themselves with raking in the shekels from a steady stream of handsome and rich extraterrestrial tourists.

After Jerry's tourist promotion had been running two years, the U.S. Post Office broke down and printed an issue of three-cent stamps commemorating the influx, showing the goddess Terra with welcoming arms open to the starred heavens. Jerry Jergins, the second advertising man in history to achieve the distinction of having Uncle Sam plug his product on a stamp, thereby entered the most select circles of his chosen profession.

Jerry bought enough of the stamps to paper the walls of his swank and spacious penthouse offices, for the benefit of the swarm of tourists who invaded the place daily during afternoon open-house hours. They all wanted to see an advertising agency; to them, this phenomenon was the essence of that primitive planet, Earth. Jerry had recorded a lecture on primitive Earth customs which issued from concealed loudspeakers, and filled display cases with exhibits of primitive Earth culture, emphasizing the aspects he felt these extraterrestrials would find most exotic.

Considering the fact that Jerry had managed to learn little about the Federated Planets that was not utterly essential to the mechanics of his advertising campaign there, he had done a pretty good job of "getting on the customer's side of the counter." Every tourist Jerry talked to had been conditioned, by some unrevealed but apparently foolproof process, not to repeat the Ambassador's error of mentioning Matter Repositors, or other aspects of life on the Federated Planets that might cause repercussions on Earth. Even tourist children couldn't be bribed with lollypops. Tourists talked a great deal, in fluent idiomatic Earth English, yet somehow said very little.

But Jerry knew at least one thing—he was stirring emotions that lay so deep under layers and layers of civilization that these shining, perfect people hadn't known they were capable of feeling them, until they visited Earth. He was getting under their smooth skins, just as surely as the monotone of a Haitian drumbeat gets under the skin of a New Yorker.

One of the display cases contained the working tools of gangsterism—sawed-off shotguns, blackjacks, a model of a bullet-proof automobile, a news photo of the St. Valentine's Day massacre, a clipping about police payoffs from houses of gambling and prostitution, another about blindness resulting from wood alcohol. The shot-glasses of authentic antique bootleg gin that stood on top the cases were often smelled but never sampled.

The second case showed a chart of fluctuations of the stock market, with an actual operating ticker in the middle. Sections of the tape were much in demand as souvenirs. But the photo of a smashed body of a once-wealthy man who jumped from his office window after losing his fortune caused the most comment. The tourists found it difficult to understand how this man could consider his life less important than his bank balance.

The largest case contained models of war weapons, a lurid painting of Pearl Harbor under aerial attack, another of the Hiroshima mushroom that ushered in the atomic age. There were gas masks, artificial limbs, a photo of a blinded veteran led by a Seeing-Eye dog. The tourists gaped at that exhibit with all the relish of Coney Island crowds visiting wax replicas of famous murder scenes.

And along the entire 40-foot wall of the reception room, a photo-mural of a ragged, depression-era breadline brooded over the sleek heads of the beautifully dressed and elaborately fed tourists.

On his way back to the office after lunch one day, Jerry spied a traffic-stopping cluster of humanity in the street outside one of the city's leading department stores. The crowd was gathered around a paddy-wagon. Never diffident, Jerry elbowed his way through the crush, to see two handsome and once well-groomed gentlemen getting a mussing up from a couple of cops. The suspects, athletic-looking characters, were putting up a good fight, and the policemen didn't like it. As Jerry watched, a billy descended on a well-barbered head, and suspect number one ceased resisting arrest.

Jerry had come into contact with enough extraterrestrials by now so that he knew a tourist when he saw one. The male tourists gave him a violent pain in the neck, but he felt somewhat responsible. He grabbed an elbow of the suspect who remained conscious.

"Give me your name, bud, and I'll bail you out. What happened?"

"Oh, we just took a few things off the counters in that store," the tourist answered. "You're very kind, but we have plenty of money for bail, thanks. Or is it a bribe you're supposed to hand them?"

"If you have plenty of money, why in hell didn't you buy the stuff, instead of stealing it?"

"We just thought we'd have a bit of a lark. New experience and all that. When on Earth, do as the Earthmen do."

"A lark!" the biggest policeman grunted. "We'll give you a lark, all right! Get in there, you!" He implemented his command with a well-placed kick in the seat of a pair of expertly tailored pants, boosting the tourist into the paddy-wagon, where his unconscious friend had already been deposited.

The siren screamed, dispersing the crowd in front of the police vehicle, and Jerry went on his way, chuckling. As he passed a hole-in-the-wall bar he knew, he decided to stop for a quick one, to settle the heavy feeling in his stomach that came from eating lobster Newburg for lunch. It wasn't a place where you'd care to take a lady, but they served an honest ounce.

As Jerry pushed through the old-fashioned swinging doors, a burst of sound greeted him. A whiskey baritone was rendering one of the unpublishable versions of "Christopher Columbo," to the accompaniment of a piano tinkle by the hired help. The customer was obviously from the other side of the tracks—from the other side of the Galaxy, in fact—and he was leaning against the piano for the simple reason that he couldn't stand up.

He wore a well-cut California-style dinner jacket, and after all night and half the day, the white gabardine was no longer white. Several drinks had been spilled on the midnight-blue flannel trousers. Only a magnificent physique distinguished him from the Earth or garden variety of drunk.

Jerry stood up to the bar, and as his eyes became accustomed to the dimness, he observed a touching—literally—scene being enacted in the darkest booth. An Earthside racetrack tout, whom Jerry recognized as one of the habitues of the place, had a gorgeous female tourist backed into a corner. She had retreated as far as the wall permitted, but he had long since caught up.

Her jaunty, elbow-length chinchilla cape lay on the wet table. Her exquisitely simple strapless dinner dress of silver lamé exposed arms and shoulders that were literally out of this world. The naked effect was relieved only by a diamond, platinum, and emerald choker. Jerry knew, though the racetrack tout probably didn't, that the priceless bauble was

Repositor-synthesized, with an Earth museum piece as a model.

It was a tossup whether the race track tout was more interested in the diamonds or the tempting flesh they adorned. The girl made no attempt to fight him off. The reason for her acquiescence was not far to seek. The glass before her contained the remains of a "Pink Lady," which tastes like an ice-cream soda and kicks like four Kentucky mules.

She moved her left hand to pick up the glass, and Jerry caught the flash of a circlet of channel-set baguette diamonds on the third finger. He concluded that she was the wife of the whiskey baritone. That worthy seemed utterly unconcerned about the whole thing, so why should Jerry interfere?

• • •

Vocabulary words:
Find these words in the section, write the sentence they are used in, and write your own definition. If you are stuck, look it up in the dictionary, but still write a definition in your own words.

repercussions
diffident
lark
habitues

Comprehension/extension questions:

What were the aliens interested in seeing?

Why did they steal merchandise from the store?

• • •

The racetrack tout left his conquest momentarily, walked over to the bar, handed the bartender a five-spot. Without comment, the bartender took down a key tagged 13 from a hook, and the turf expert pocketed it. There was a dingy sign reading "Hotel" outside; Jerry had always supposed the floors above contained equally dingy furnished rooms.

The beautiful tourist's silver heels mounted the back stairs unsteadily. The tout was half steering her, half supporting her. The man was sober enough to know exactly what he was doing. When she came back down those stairs, she would be minus not only her virtue, but her diamond necklace as well.

"Oh, he knew the world was round-o, that sailors could be found-o," the whiskey baritone sang lustily.

Jerry left the saloon with a bad taste in his mouth. As he passed through the electric-eye doorway of his office suite, he had the impression that the too perfect inhabitants of all the color advertising pages he had turned out in past years had suddenly come to life. Handsome tourists were moving, in chattering groups, from one display case to another.

Their chatter, as usual, gave him few clues. He still harbored a suspicion that on their home planets, these lovely people might be symbiotes in the bodies of lower animals, or loathsome but intellectual worms. But he never had any success when he tried to pump them about whether they were like Earth inhabitants at home, or were issued these magnificent bodies and faces along with their passports to Earth.

His unreasoning dislike of the males was undoubtedly part jealousy, for they were all tall, handsome, well-dressed, and athletic enough to be signed *en masse* by Hollywood. But the universal utter perfection of limb, features, and complexion, was not at all repulsive in the female. It was quite decorative to have a whole chorus of toothsome girls in Paris gowns cluttering up the office.

Jerry had never seen one of them use a lipstick, rouge, or an eyebrow pencil. The cosmetic business was one of the few that had not profited from the tourist trade, except insofar as lady tourists bought costly perfumes, and Earthgirls strove to mimic the natural— or unnatural—coloring of the fair visitors. A few tourists brought their children along, and here the firm, rosy, unblemished skin was in its proper element. Tourist children were not one whit more cherubic than well-favored children of Earth.

A guide from the Conducted Tours Company arrived to round up a batch of tourists, for a visit to the local jails, flop-houses, and gambling dens. He announced they would go by bus, and the horrified yet delighted whoops that greeted this news reminded Jerry of a Boston society dowager who had just been invited to ride on a camel.

As the crowd trickled out the doors, a lovely vision in platinum blonde laid a slender hand on Jerry's arm.

"Are you really the man who first thought of inviting us to this quaint and delightful planet?" she gushed.

"I guess I am, lady. How do you like it?"

"Oh, it's so primitive! So elemental! Everybody used to think visiting backward planets was dull and scholarly stuff. It took *you* to show us how thrilling and exciting it can be!"

"I'm glad to hear you say that. Some of the tourists are complaining that Earth isn't as primitive as the Tourist Bureau advertising makes it out to be."

"Oh, you *do* exaggerate a wee, tiny bit, but it's all in good fun, isn't it? On the whole, I'm not disappointed—especially not in the *men*!" She fluttered eyelashes, so long and dark that they looked artificial, at him.

"The men?" Jerry asked blankly.

"Oh, come, come!" the platinum blonde breathed throatily into his ear. "Don't pretend to be so innocent! You must have heard of the simply *terrific* reputation Earthmen have acquired on other planets as masterful lovers!"

"It's news to me," Jerry admitted, "but it sounds like a good drawing card. I'll try to work something like that into our ads."

"Always thinking about business, aren't you? Why don't you think of something else, for a change? Me, for instance. Don't you feel a little bit sorry for a girl like me, with nothing but perfectly civilized men to go home to?" the girl pouted invitingly.

Jerry found himself, by imperceptible stages, being backed into a corner. Well, well, he thought. Perhaps he'd been too harsh in judging that racetrack tout.

"Since you mention it," Jerry said, "I'm not averse to playing the role of Galactic beachboy."

"What does a beachboy do?"

"I'd blush to explain it verbally to a girl unaccustomed to primitive Earth customs, but I'm pretty good at sign language. How about dinner tonight?"

"Well… if you'll let me pay the check. I do so adore this amazing Earth custom of exchanging food for little slips of paper."

"The pleasure is all yours, sister. See you at the Ritz main dining room—eight o'clock. Soup and fish. Afterward, we'll look at my photo-murals. Now toddle along, baby, if you want to catch the bus to see those hoboes."

Jerry was walking on the Milky Way. Aside from the profits, this job had its esthetic side, he decided. His exuberance was slightly dampened by the grim expression on his secretary's face.

"A very important man has been waiting to see you," she said disapprovingly. "I sent him into your office. The least I could do was put him where he wouldn't have to smell all the perfume these brazen tourist women use. It's enough to make a person ill!"

In the visitor's chair before Jerry's mother-of-pearl inlaid desk, the Ambassador from Outer Space was waiting, staring morosely at the endlessly repeated welcoming goddess Terra on Jerry's wall stamp collection.

"Well, as I live and breathe!" Jerry exclaimed, "a real, live B-29 pilot! Welcome to my humble grass shack! Scotch? Cigar? What can I do for you?"

"You can put out your bonfire, cannibal," the Ambassador said, gruffly. "I think I've stewed enough."

"Why are you tough, then?" Jerry asked. "At me, I mean. I thought I was your best friend in this here jungle. Didn't I do you a favor once, Mr. Ambassador?"

"A *favor*? I paid you well for it! Not only in money, but by getting advertising space for your precious Tourist Bureau on the Federated Planets. I never thought it would lead to this!"

"You thought my copy wouldn't pull, eh? Not even after I'd demonstrated I could make Earth opinion do a flip-flop on that Matter Repositor deal?"

"Oh, I was quite sure you could manipulate Earthmen. That's your job. But I didn't believe our people would respond in such numbers to an appeal to primitive emotions!"

"You weren't alone in that," Jerry said smugly. "Some very prominent members of our organization wanted to make the campaign more civilized. I showed them where they were wrong. Can't you see that your people are fed up with civilization, right up to their pretty white necks? The very essence of Earth's appeal to them is that a trip here gives them a chance to relax their ethics, to play at going native."

"Don't rub it in!" The Ambassador shuddered.

"It's nothing new. Tourists have always kicked up their heels. Guess what I saw while I was out to lunch. The cops grabbed a couple of your boys for shoplifting! They thought it was such fun to ride in the paddy-wagon. Back home, of course, they wouldn't think of repositing anything they weren't supposed to, but on Earth it's different."

"And for monkeyshines like that," the Ambassador growled, "I am driven half crazy working out sleep-record courses. 'Idioms of Earth English'—'What Not to Say on Backward Planets and Why'—'Earth Fashion

Guide, What You Can Buy There and What to Reposit.' Bah! I'm supposed to be a diplomat, not a fashion adviser!"

"Why don't you hire some help?" Jerry suggested.

"I have. I've hired a whole staff, with offices in all major Earth cities, to exchange platinum, bullion, and precious stones for Earth currencies. It's a man-sized job, I can tell you, to keep Earth currencies stable under this load!"

"You're doing a very good job," Jerry said, soothingly.

"You know what one of our citizens asked me yesterday? How she could get a marriage license! Your officials had turned her down, because she'd been conditioned not to mention her birthplace and age. Mind you, a citizen of the Federated Planets wanted to marry an Earthman and live on this raw, Galactic frontier the rest of her life! Why, we don't even know whether the races can cross-breed!"

"That should be looked into," Jerry agreed.

"What are you trying to do?" the Ambassador demanded, "Drag the citizens of the Federated Planets down to the level of your jungle? You blithely assume those two shoplifters can be trusted with Matter Repositors when they get back home, but I'm not so sure. We haven't any jails to toss them into, but we may have to establish some. Matter-Repositor-proof jails!"

"That's your problem," Jerry said. "All I'm trying to do is make some money for myself and, other businessmen on Earth. Which I'm doing, thank you. And I doubt that you could stop me, at this point. Your citizens would raise quite a howl if my ads stopped appearing in the information bulletins."

"Money!" the Ambassador exclaimed, "All you Earthmen think about is money!" He leaned over Jerry's desk. "What if you could reposit the money—the gold, that is—without all the work you have to put into entertaining these tourists?"

"Hmm," Jerry said, thinking of his date for that evening, and other equally lovely tourists. "Money isn't the only thing in life. And don't forget the income tax. I've got to have some deductible expenses."

"Knowing you, I'd bet you could figure out some way of handling that little detail."

"What's your proposition?"

"Two years ago, you came to my office, wanting to import Matter Repositors. I told you Earth's civilization wasn't ready for them."

"We still aren't, according to what you say about our avaricious instincts."

"No, you're not. But you have methods of manipulating public opinion and attitudes that are far more advanced than those found on other planets."

"So you admit that Earth is advanced in something!" Jerry said happily.

"How would you like to have the name of Jerry Jergins go down in your history as the originator of the most significant public-relations campaign ever undertaken on this planet?" the Ambassador asked, temptingly. "You can handle it, if any man on Earth can."

"Softsoaping me again! What's the campaign? I'll listen to it, but I don't know whether I'll buy it."

"Your job would be to get Earth's psychology and sociology ready for the Matter Repositor."

Jerry reflected. "You mean I'd have to eliminate war, supplement the Voice of America, and so on? I'd have certain advantages over the Voice of America, at that. I wouldn't have a bunch of politicians playing football with my appropriations."

"This campaign would have to go further and deeper than the Voice of America. You might call it the Voice of Conscience. Its aim would be to make every human being on Earth care more about the welfare of his fellow-man than he cares about his own."

"A couple of thousand years back," Jerry said, soberly, "a better Promoter than I tried to put that idea across. The campaign He started is still running. It's taken hold in some quarters, but I wouldn't say public acceptance is anything like worldwide yet."

"Then you don't think you can do it?" the Ambassador asked, his eagerness somewhat deflated.

"I'm not committing myself to whether I could or couldn't. I could put the Ten Commandments on an international hookup. Thou shalt not steal. Thou shalt not covet thy neighbor his goods. I could get Walt Disney to dramatize the golden rule."

"Ah, I see you have some ideas for the copy already," the Ambassador said. "I thought I could get you interested in it. Then you'll sign a contract?"

"No," Jerry said, briefly and definitely.

"Now, wait a minute, Mr. Jergins," the Ambassador protested. "Why do you suddenly become blunt and unqualified? Do you realize what I'm offering you? In return for ceasing this tourist promotion, I'm offering you the invention that obsolesces all others—the Matter Repositor!"

Jerry stood up and placed the palms of his hands flat on his desk. "I told you that you'd learn something in our primitive jungle, Mr. Ambassador. Well, this is it. We may be mechanical morons, according to your standards, but we naked savages can produce anything we need. Since we've corrected the misconception that what Earth produces isn't good enough for Earthmen, and whipped up a tourist trade, business is booming. And when it booms, we can distribute those Earth products in a way that suits us pretty well. A primitive way, you may think, but one that is adapted to the unfortunate circumstance that we aren't a bunch of little tin saints living in an ideal world.

"I asked you for Matter Repositors once, and you were wise enough to turn me down. I'm glad you did. They'd cause us more trouble than the atomic bomb. We don't want the damn things. Do you understand that?"

On sudden impulse, Jerry strode across his office. There stood a large and brilliantly colored object, jarring oddly with the other furniture. Sometimes at a loss to spend his newly acquired wealth, Jerry had yielded, a month or so before, to a desire conceived in childhood to own a real honest-to-goodness juke box.

Jerry fished in his pocket for a nickel, deposited it in the slot, pushed button seven. Loud, tinny, and offensively blatant, the strains of "I Don't Wanna Leave the Congo" filled the office, effectively drowning out any further remarks the Ambassador from Outer Space might have wished to make.

"If you'll pardon me," Jerry shouted over the din, "I have some arrow heads to chip—and a potential extraterrestrial mate to woo with a quaint tribal ritual we call dating on Earth."

• • •

Vocabulary words:
Find these words in the section, write the sentence they are used in, and write your own definition. If you are stuck, look it up in the dictionary, but still write a definition in your own words.

symbiotes
dowager
averse
avaricious

Comprehension/extension questions:

What do the aliens like about earth?

Who is the 'better Promoter' Jergins is speaking of?

How are the aliens changing earth? How is earth changing the aliens?

The Pilot and the Bushman, by Sylvia Jacobs, Published August 1951

Sylvia Jacobs published a few short stories in the 1950s.

I AM A NUCLEUS

By STEPHEN BARR
Illustrated by GAUGHAN

No doubt whatever about it, I had the Indian sign on me... my comfortably untidy world had suddenly turned into a monstrosity of order!

Editor's note: Language in this story may be offensive to some readers. Review before student.

When I got home from the office, I was not so much tired as beaten down, but the effect is similar. I let myself into the apartment, which had an absentee-wife look, and took a cold shower. The present downtown temperature, according to the radio, was eighty-seven degrees, but according to my Greenwich Village thermometer, it was ninety-six. I got dressed and went into the living room, and wished ardently that my wife Molly were here to tell me why the whole place looked so woebegone.

What do they do, I asked myself, that I have left undone? I've vacuumed the carpet, I've dusted and I've straightened the cushions…. Ah! The ashtrays. I emptied them, washed them and put them back, but still the place looked wife-deserted.

It had been a bad day; I had forgotten to wind the alarm clock, so I'd had to hurry to make a story conference at one of the TV studios I write for. I didn't notice the impending rain storm and had no umbrella when I reached the sidewalk, to find myself confronted with an almost tropical downpour. I would have turned back, but a taxi came up and a woman got out, so I dashed through the rain and got in.

"Madison and Fifty-fourth," I said.

"Right," said the driver, and I heard the starter grind, and then go on grinding. After some futile efforts, he turned to me. "Sorry, Mac. You'll have to find another cab. Good hunting."

If possible, it was raining still harder. I opened my newspaper over my hat and ran for the subway: three blocks. Whizzing traffic held me up at each crossing and I was soaked when I reached the platform, just in time to miss the local. After an abnormal delay, I got one which exactly missed the express at Fourteenth Street. The same thing happened at both ends of the crosstown shuttle, but I found the rain had stopped when I got out at Fifty-first and Lexington.

As I walked across to Madison Avenue, I passed a big excavation where they were getting ready to put up a new office building. There was the usual crowd of buffs watching the digging machines and, in particular, a man with a pneumatic drill who was breaking up some hard-packed clay. While I looked, a big lump of it fell away, and for an instant I was able to see something that looked like a chunk of dirty glass, the size of an old-fashioned hatbox. It glittered brilliantly in the sunlight, and then his chattering drill hit it.

There was a faint bang and the thing disintegrated. It knocked him on his back, but he got right up and I realized he was not hurt. At the moment of the explosion—if so feeble a thing can be called one—I felt something sting my face and, on touching it, found blood on my hand. I mopped at it with my handkerchief but, though slight, the bleeding would not stop, so I went into a drugstore and bought some pink adhesive which I put on the tiny cut. When I got to the studio, I found that I had missed the story conference.

During the day, by actual count, I heard the phrase "I'm just spitballing" eight times, and another Madison Avenue favorite, "The whole ball of wax," twelve times. However, my story had been accepted without change because nobody had noticed my absence from the conference room. There you have what is known as the advertising world, the advertising game or the advertising racket, depending upon which rung of the ladder you have achieved.

The subway gave a repeat performance going home, and as I got to the apartment house we live in, the cop on the afternoon beat was standing there talking to the doorman.

He said, "Hello, Mr. Graham. I guess you must have just have missed it at your office building." I looked blank and he explained, "We just heard it a little while ago: all six elevators in your building jammed at the same time. Sounds crazy. I guess you just missed it."

Anything can happen in advertising, I thought. "That's right, Danny, I just missed it," I said, and went on in.

Psychiatry tells us that some people are accident-prone; I, on the other hand, seemed recently to be coincidence-prone, fluke-happy, and except for the alarm clock, I'd had no control over what had been going on.

I went into our little kitchen to make a drink and reread the directions Molly had left, telling me how to get along by myself until she got back from her mother's in Oyster Bay, a matter of ten days. How to make coffee, how to open a can, whom to call if I took sick and such. My wife used to be a trained nurse and she is quite convinced that I cannot take a breath without her. She is right, but not for the reasons she supposes.

I opened the refrigerator to get some ice and saw another notice: "When you take out the Milk or Butter, Put it Right Back. And Close the Door, too."

Intimidated, I took my drink into the living room and sat down in front of the typewriter. As I stared at the novel that was to liberate me from Madison Avenue, I noticed a mistake and picked up a pencil. When I put it down, it rolled off the desk, and with my eyes on the manuscript, I groped under the chair for it. Then I looked down. The pencil was standing on its end.

• • •

Vocabulary words:
Find these words in the section, write the sentence they are used in, and write your own definition. If you are stuck, look it up in the dictionary, but still write a definition in your own words.

absentee
ardently
excavation

Comprehension/extension questions:

Why did he have to wind the alarm clock?

What does his wife think of his living skills?

• • •

There, I thought to myself, is that one chance in a million we hear about, and picked up the pencil. I turned back to my novel and drank some of the highball in hopes of inspiration and surcease from the muggy heat, but nothing came. I went back and read the whole chapter to try to get a forward momentum, but came to a dead stop at the last sentence.

Damn the heat, damn the pencil, damn Madison Avenue and advertising. My drink was gone and I went back to the kitchen and read Molly's notes again to see if they would be like a letter from her. I noticed one that I had missed, pinned to the door of the dumbwaiter: "Garbage picked up at 6:30 AM so the idea is to Put it here the night before. I love you." What can you do when the girl loves you?

I made another drink and went and stared out of the living room window at the roof opposite. The sun was out again and a man with a stick was exercising his flock of pigeons. They wheeled in a circle, hoping to be allowed to perch, but were not allowed to.

Pigeons fly as a rule in formation and turn simultaneously, so that their wings all catch the sunlight at the same time. I was thinking about this decorative fact when I saw that as they were making a turn, they seemed to bunch up together. By some curious chance, they all wanted the same place in the sky to turn in, and several collided and fell.

The man was as surprised as I and went to one of the dazed birds and picked it up. He stood there shaking his head from side to side, stroking its feathers.

My speculations about this peculiar aerial traffic accident were interrupted by loud voices in the hallway. Since our building is usually very well-behaved, I was astonished to hear what sounded like an incipient free-for-all, and among the angry voices I recognized that of my neighbor, Nat, a very quiet guy who works on a newspaper and has never, to my knowledge, given wild parties, particularly in the late afternoon.

"You can't say a thing like that to me!" I heard him shout. "I tell you I got that deck this afternoon and they weren't opened till we started to play!"

Several other loud voices started at the same time.

"Nobody gets five straight flushes in a row!"

"Yeah, and only when you were dealer!"

The tone of the argument was beginning to get ugly, and I opened the door to offer Nat help if he needed it. There were four men confronting him, evidently torn between the desire to make an angry exit and the impulse to stay and beat him up. His face was furiously red and he looked stunned.

"Here!" he said, holding out a deck of cards, "For Pete's sake, look at 'em yourselves if you think they're marked!"

The nearest man struck them up from his hand. "Okay, Houdini! So they're not marked! All I know is five straight...."

His voice trailed away. He and the others stared at the scattered cards on the floor. About half were face down, as might be expected, and the rest face up—all red.

Someone must have rung, because at that moment the elevator arrived and the four men, with half-frightened, incredulous looks, and in silence, got in and were taken down. My friend stood looking at the neatly arranged cards.

"Judas!" he said, and started to pick them up. "Will you look at that! My God, what a session...."

I helped him and said to come in for a drink and tell me all about it, but I had an idea what I would hear.

After a while, he calmed down, but he still seemed dazed.

"Never seen anything to equal it," he said. "Wouldn't have believed it. Those guys *didn't* believe it. Every round normal, nothing unusual about the hands—three of a kind, a low straight, that sort of thing and one guy got queens over tens, until it gets to be *my* deal. Brother! Straight flush to the king—every time! And each time, somebody else has four aces...."

He started to sweat again, so I got up to fix him another drink. There was one quart of club soda left, but when I tried to open it, the top broke and glass chips got into the bottle.

"I'll have to go down for more soda," I said.

"I'll come, too. I need air."

At the delicatessen on the corner, the man gave me three bottles in what must have been a wet bag, because as he handed them to me over the top of the cold-meat display, the bottom gave and they fell onto the tile floor. None of them broke, although the fall must have been from at least five feet. Nat was too wound up in his thoughts to notice and I was getting used to miracles. We left the proprietor with his mouth open and met Danny, the cop, looking in at the door, also with his mouth open.

On the sidewalk, a man walking in front of Nat stooped suddenly to tie his shoe and Nat, to avoid bumping him, stepped off the curb and a taxi swerved to avoid Nat. The street was still wet and the taxi skidded, its rear end lightly flipping the front of one of those small foreign cars, which was going rather fast. It turned sideways and, without any side-slip, went right up the stoop of a brownstone opposite, coming to rest with its nose inside the front door, which a man opened at that moment.

The sight of this threw another driver into a skid, and when he and the taxi had stopped sliding around, they were face to face, arranged crosswise to the street. This gave them exactly no room to move either forward or backward, for the car had its back to a hydrant and the taxi to a lamp.

Although rather narrow, this is a two-way street, and in no time at all, traffic was stacked up from both directions as far as the avenues. Everyone was honking his horn.

Danny was furious—more so when he tried to put through a call to his station house from the box opposite.

It was out of order.

• • •

Vocabulary words:
Find these words in the section, write the sentence they are used in, and write your own definition. If you are stuck, look it up in the dictionary, but still write a definition in your own words.

surcease
wheeled
incredulous
Comprehension/extension questions:

What strange things did the narrator notice happening around him?

• • •

Upstairs, the wind was blowing into the apartment and I closed the windows, mainly to shut out the tumult and the shouting. Nat had brightened up considerably.

"I'll stay for one more drink and then I'm due at the office," he said. "You know, I think this would make an item for the paper." He grinned and nodded toward the pandemonium.

When he was gone, I noticed it was getting dark and turned on the desk lamp. Then I saw the curtains. They were all tied in knots, except one. That was tied in three knots.

All *right*, I told myself, it was the wind. But I felt the time had come for me to get expert advice, so I went to the phone to call McGill. McGill is an assistant professor of mathematics at a university uptown and lives near us. He is highly imaginative, but we believe he knows everything.

When I picked up the receiver, the line sounded dead and I thought, *more* trouble. Then I heard a man cough and I said hello. McGill's voice said, "Alec? You must have picked up the receiver just as we were connected. That's a damn funny coincidence."

"Not in the least," I said. "Come on over here. I've got something for you to work on."

"Well, as a matter of fact, I was calling up to ask you and Molly—"

"Molly's away for the week. Can you get over here quick? It's urgent."

"At once," he said, and hung up.

While I waited, I thought I might try getting down a few paragraphs of my novel—perhaps something would come now. It did, but as I came to a point where I was about to put down the word "agurgling," I decided it was too reminiscent of Gilbert and Sullivan, and stopped at the letter "R." Then I saw that I had unaccountably hit all four keys one step to the side of the correct ones, and tore out the page, with my face red.

This was absolutely not my day.

"Well," McGill said, "nothing you've told me is impossible or supernatural. Just very, very improbable. In fact, the odds against that poker game alone would lead me to suspect Nat, well as I know him. It's all those other things...."

He got up and walked over to the window and looked at the hot twilight while I waited. Then he turned around; he had a look of concern.

"Alec, you're a reasonable guy, so I don't think you'll take offense at what I'm going to say. What you have told me is so impossibly unlikely, and the odds against it so astronomical, that I must take the view that you're either stringing me or you're subject to a delusion." I started to get up and expostulate, but he motioned me back. "I know, but don't you see that that is far more likely than…." He stopped and shook his head. Then he brightened. "I have an idea. Maybe we can have a demonstration."

He thought for a tense minute and snapped his fingers. "Have you any change on you?"

"Why, yes," I said. "Quite a bit." I reached into my pocket. There must have been nearly two dollars in silver and pennies. "Do you think they'll each have the same date, perhaps?"

"Did you accumulate all that change today?"

"No. During the week."

He shook his head. "In that case, no. Discounting the fact that you could have prearranged it, if my dim provisional theory is right, that would be *actually* impossible. It would involve time-reversal. I'll tell you about it later. No, just throw down the change. Let's see if they all come up heads."

I moved away from the carpet and tossed the handful of coins onto the floor. They clattered and bounced—and bounced together—and stacked themselves into a neat pile.

I looked at McGill. His eyes were narrowed. Without a word, he took a handful of coins from his own pocket and threw them.

These coins didn't stack. They just fell into an exactly straight line, the adjacent ones touching.

"Well," I said, "what more do you want?"

"Great Scott," he said, and sat down. "I suppose you know that there are two great apparently opposite principles governing the Universe—random and design. The sands on the beach are an example of random distribution and life is an example of design. The motions of the particles of a gas are what we call random, but there are so many of them, we treat them statistically and derive the Second Law of Thermodynamics—quite reliable. It isn't theoretically hard-and-fast; it's just a matter of extreme probability. Now life, on the other hand, seems not to depend on probability at all; actually, it goes against it. Or you might say it is certainly not an accidental manifestation."

"Do you mean," I asked in some confusion, "that some form of life is controlling the coins and—the other things?"

He shook his head. "No. All I mean is that improbable things usually have improbable explanations. When I see a natural law being broken, I don't say to myself, 'Here's a miracle.' I revise my version of the book of rules. Something—I don't know what—is going on, and it seems to involve probability, and it seems to center around you. Were you still in that building when the elevators stuck? Or near it?"

"I guess I must have been. It happened just after I left."

"Hm. You're the center, all right. But why?"

"Center of what?" I asked. "I feel as though I were the center of an electrical storm. Something has it in for me!"

McGill grinned. "Don't be superstitious. And especially don't be anthropomorphic."

"Well, if it's the opposite of random, it's got to be a form of life."

"On what basis? All we know for certain is that random motions are being rearranged. A crystal, for example, is not life, but it's a non-random arrangement of particles.... I wonder." He had a faraway, frowning look.

I was beginning to feel hungry and the drinks had worn off.

"Let's go out and eat," I said, "There's not a damn thing in the kitchen and I'm not allowed to cook. Only eggs and coffee."

We put on our hats and went down to the street. From either end, we could hear wrecking trucks towing away the stalled cars. There were, by this time, a number of harassed cops directing the maneuver and we heard one of them say to Danny, "I don't know what the hell's going on around here. Every goddam car's got something the matter with it. They can't none of them back out for one reason or another. Never seen anything like it."

Near us, two pedestrians were doing a curious little two-step as they tried to pass one another; as soon as one of them moved aside to let the other pass, the other would move to the same side. They both had embarrassed grins on their faces, but before long their grins were replaced by looks of suspicion and then determination.

"All right, smart guy!" they shouted in unison, and barged ahead, only to collide. They backed off and threw simultaneous punches which met in mid-air. Then began one of the most remarkable bouts ever witnessed—a fight in which fist hit fist but never anything else, until both champions backed away undefeated, muttering identical excuses and threats.

• • •

Vocabulary words:
Find these words in the section, write the sentence they are used in, and write your own definition. If you are stuck, look it up in the dictionary, but still write a definition in your own words.

pandemonium
supernatural
astronomical
provisional

Comprehension/extension questions:

What word did he accidentally type?

What would you do if all of these coincidences were happening around you? How would you feel about it?

• • •

Danny appeared at that moment. His face was dripping. "You all right, Mr. Graham?" he asked. "I don't know what's going on around here, but ever since I came on this afternoon, things are going crazy. Bartley!" he shouted—he could succeed as a hog-caller. "Bring those dames over here!"

Three women in a confused wrangle, with their half-open umbrellas intertwined, were brought across the street, which meant climbing over fenders. Bartley, a fine young patrolman, seemed selfconscious; the ladies seemed not to be.

"All right, now, Mrs. Mac-Philip!" one of them said. "Leave go of my umbrella and we'll say no more about it!"

"And so now it's Missus Mac-Philip, is it?" said her adversary.

The third, a younger one with her back turned to us, her umbrella also caught in the tangle, pulled at it in a tentative way, at which the other two glared at her. She turned her head away and tried to let go, but the handle was caught in her glove. She looked up and I saw it was Molly. My nurse-wife.

"Oh, Alec!" she said, and managed to detach herself. "Are you all right?" Was *I* all right!

"Molly! What are you doing here?"

"I was so worried, and when I saw all this, I didn't know what to think." She pointed to the stalled cars. "Are you really all right?"

"Of course I'm all right. But why...."

"The Oyster Bay operator said someone kept dialing and dialing Mother's number and there wasn't anyone on the line, so then she had it traced and it came from our phone here. I kept calling up, but I only got a busy signal. Oh, dear, are you *sure* you're all right?"

I put my arm around her and glanced at McGill. He had an inward look. Then I caught Danny's eye. It had a thoughtful, almost suspicious cast to it.

"Trouble does seem to follow you, Mr. Graham," was all he said.

When we got upstairs, I turned to McGill. "Explain to Molly," I said. "And incidentally to me. I'm not properly briefed yet."

He did so, and when he got to the summing up, I had the feeling she was a jump ahead of him.

"In other words, you think it's something organic?"

"Well," McGill said, "I'm trying to think of anything else it might be. I'm not doing so well," he confessed.

"But so far as I can see," Molly answered, "it's mere probability, and without any overall pattern."

"Not quite. It has a center. Alec is the center."

Molly looked at me with a curious expression for a moment. "Do you *feel* all right, darling?" she asked me. I nodded brightly. "You'll think this silly of me," she went on to McGill, "but why isn't it something like an overactive poltergeist?"

"Pure concept," he said. "No genuine evidence."

"Magnetism?"

"Absolutely not. For one thing, most of the objects affected weren't magnetic—and don't forget magnetism is a force, not a form of energy, and a great deal of energy has been involved. I admit the energy has mainly been supplied by the things themselves, but in a magnetic field, all you'd get would be stored kinetic energy, such as when a piece of iron moves to a magnet or a line of force. Then it would just stay there, like a rundown clock weight. These things do a lot more than that—they go on moving."

"Why did you mention a crystal before? Why not a life-form?"

"Only an analogy," said McGill. "A crystal resembles life in that it has a definite shape and exhibits growth, but that's all. I'll agree this—thing—has no discernible shape and motion *is* involved, but plants don't move and amebas have no shape. Then a crystal feeds, but it does not convert what it feeds on; it merely rearranges it into a non-random pattern. In this case, it's rearranging random motions and it has a nucleus and it seems to be growing—at least in what you might call improbability."

Molly frowned. "Then what *is* it? What's it made of?"

"I should say it was made of the motions. There's a similar idea about the atom. Another thing that's like a crystal is that it appears to be forming around a nucleus not of its own material—the way a speck of sand thrown into a supersaturated solution becomes the nucleus of crystallization."

"Sounds like the pearl in an oyster," Molly said, and gave me an impertinent look.

"Why," I asked McGill, "did you say the coins couldn't have the same date? I mean apart from the off chance I got them that way."

"Because I don't think this thing got going before today and everything that's happened can all be described as improbable motions here and now. The dates were already there, and to change them would require retroactive action, reversing time. That's out, in my book. That telephone now—"

The doorbell rang. We were not surprised to find it was the telephone repairman. He took the set apart and clucked like a hen.

"I guess you dropped it on the floor, mister," he said with strong disapproval.

"Certainly not," I said. "Is it broken?"

"Not exactly *broken*, but—" He shook his head and took it apart some more.

McGill went over and they discussed the problem in undertones. Finally the man left and Molly called her mother to reassure her. McGill tried to explain to me what had happened with the phone.

"You must have joggled something loose. And then you replaced the receiver in such a way that the contact wasn't quite open."

"But for Pete's sake, Molly says the calls were going on for a long time! I phoned you only a short time ago and it must have taken her nearly two hours to get here from Oyster Bay."

"Then you must have done it twice and the vibrations in the floor—something like that—just happened to cause the right induction impulses. Yes, I know how you feel," he said, seeing my expression. "It's beginning to bear down."

Molly was through telephoning and suggested going out for dinner. I was so pleased to see her that I'd forgotten all about being hungry.

"I'm in no mood to cook," she said. "Let's get away from all this."

McGill raised an eyebrow. "If all this, as you call it, will let us."

In the lobby, we ran into Nat, looking smug in a journalistic way.

"I've been put on the story—who could be better?—I live here. So far, I don't quite get what's been happening. I've been talking to Danny, but he didn't say much. I got the feeling he thinks you're involved in some mystical, Hibernian way. Hello, McGill, what's with you?"

"He's got a theory," said Molly. "Come and eat with us and he'll tell you all about it."

Since we decided on an air-conditioned restaurant nearby on Sixth Avenue, we walked. The jam of cars didn't seem to be any less than before and we saw Danny again. He was talking to a police lieutenant, and when he caught sight of us, he said something that made the lieutenant look at us with interest. Particularly at me.

"If you want your umbrella, Mrs. Graham," Danny said, "it's at the station house. What there's left of it, that is."

Molly thanked him and there was a short pause, during which I felt the speculative regard of the lieutenant. I pulled out a packet of cigarettes, which I had opened, as always, by tearing off the top. I happened to have it upside down and all the cigarettes fell out. Before I could move my foot to obliterate what they had spelled out on the sidewalk, the two cops saw it. The lieutenant gave me a hard look, but said nothing. I quickly kicked the insulting cigarettes into the gutter.

When we got to the restaurant, it was crowded but cool—although it didn't stay cool for long. We sat down at a side table near the door and ordered Tom Collinses as we looked at the menu. Sitting at the next table were a fat lady, wearing a very long, brilliant green evening gown, and a dried-up sour-looking man in a tux. When the waiter returned, they preempted him and began ordering dinner fussily: cold cuts for the man, and vichyssoise, lobster salad and strawberry parfait for the fat lady.

I tasted my drink. It was most peculiar; salt seemed to have been used instead of sugar. I mentioned this and my companions tried theirs, and made faces.

The waiter was concerned and apologetic, and took the drinks back to the bar across the room. The bartender looked over at us and tasted one of the drinks. Then he dumped them in his sink with a puzzled expression and made a new batch. After shaking this up, he set out a row of glasses, put ice in them and began to pour.

That is to say he tilted the shaker over the first one, but nothing came out. He bumped it against the side of the bar and tried again. Still nothing. Then he took off the top and pried into it with his pick, his face pink with exasperation.

I had the impression that the shaker had frozen solid. Well, ice *is* a crystal, I thought to myself.

The other bartender gave him a fresh shaker, but the same thing happened, and I saw no more because the customers sitting at the bar crowded around in front of him, offering advice. Our waiter came back, baffled, saying he'd have the drinks in a moment, and went to the kitchen. When he returned, he had madame's vichyssoise and some rolls, which he put down, and then went to the bar, where the audience had grown larger.

Molly lit a cigarette and said, "I suppose this is all part of it, Alec. Incidentally, it seems to be getting warmer in here."

It was, and I had the feeling the place was quieter— a background noise had stopped. It dawned on me that I no longer heard the faint hum of the air-conditioner over the door, and as I started to say so, I made a gesture toward it. My hand collided with Molly's when she tapped her cigarette over the ashtray, and the cigarette landed in the neighboring vichyssoise.

"Hey! What's the idea?" snarled the sour-looking man.

"I'm terribly sorry," I said. "It was an accident. I—"

"Throwing cigarettes at people!" the fat lady said.

"I really didn't mean to," I began again, getting up. There must have been a hole in the edge of their tablecloth which one of my cuff buttons caught in, because as I stepped out from between the closely set tables, I pulled everything—tablecloth, silver, water glasses, ashtrays and the vichyssoise-à-la-nicotine—onto the floor.

The fat lady surged from the banquette and slapped me meatily. The man licked his thumb and danced as boxers are popularly supposed to do. The owner of the place, a man with thick black eyebrows, hustled toward us with a determined manner. I tried to explain what had happened, but I was outshouted, and the owner frowned darkly.

One of the waiters came up to the owner and tapped him on the shoulder and started to tell him about the air-conditioner, thus creating a momentary diversion, which did not, however, include the fat lady.

"He must be drunk!" she told her companion, who nodded contemptuously. A man carrying a stepladder came down the aisle from the back, his eye on the air-conditioner, but not, it seemed, on the stepladder, which bumped the owner of the restaurant on the shoulder just as he was turning back to me.

It was not a hard bump, but it threw him off balance, so that he more or less embraced the waiter. Then he turned around and it was obvious he thought I had struck him. The room was now divided into two groups: ourselves and our audience, and those who were too far away or intent on other matters to have noticed the fracas, the chief of these being the man with the stepladder, who was paying undivided attention to the air-conditioner. The owner was very angry with me.

"Mister, I think *you'd* better leave!" he said.

"He will not!" Molly said. "It was an accident, and *you*," she added to the fat lady who was about to interrupt, "keep quiet! We'll buy you some more soup!"

"Maybe it was an accident like you say," the owner declared, "but no one's going to push me when my back is turned! Out you go, mister! The drinks are on the house."

"We haven't had any drinks yet," I said. "There was salt in them."

"What d'you mean, salt? My bartenders—"

The air-conditioner suddenly let out a loud whirring and I glanced up. The stepladder which the man was on began to slide open like an acrobatic dancer doing a split. I stepped past the angry restaurateur and put out my hand to stop it, but as I did, the extension-bar that was supposed to hold it together parted and it came down with a rush, knocking over several tables. The repairman pulled part of the works out with him as he fell and the fan-belt broke. The motor raced and black smoke poured out.

"What're you trying to *do*!" the owner yelled at me over the loud whine of the machinery. "Goddam it, haven't you done *enough* already?"

I took two steps back, in dismay at what I was accused of, and stepped on the skirt of the fat lady's green evening gown. She in turn took two steps and was, as it were, laid bare.

The previous hubbub was as nothing to what now resulted and the smoke was becoming thicker. Then the door opened and, to my horror, Danny and his lieutenant came in, and I was the first thing their eyes fastened on. Everyone started shouting at once and pointing at me.

Then the sprinkler system went on.

• • •

Vocabulary words:

Find these words in the section, write the sentence they are used in, and write your own definition. If you are stuck, look it up in the dictionary, but still write a definition in your own words.

poltergeist
improbability
mystical
fracas

Comprehension/extension questions:

What do you think the cigarettes spelled out?

How can he stop the accidents from happening? What would you do?

• • •

The cell was clean, although very hot, and I was not treated badly. There was, in fact, an air of superstitious respect, almost. A cop gave me some magazines and, against regulations, a late paper, but it was not late enough to carry the story of the restaurant mob-scene. In it, however, was a garbled account of our traffic jam and a reference to the six elevators simultaneously and unaccountably stuck in the I.T.V. Building, but no connection was suggested.

My mind was in too much of an uproar to read, and I paced up and down. It seemed hours since McGill had called my lawyer Vinelli; some fantastic mishap must be holding him up, I thought. Then I happened to bump into the door of the cell and found the lock hadn't caught.

More of the same! But there didn't seem any point in trying to escape. Where would I go? Besides, I would have to leave through the desk room, where there would be at least the desk lieutenant and a sergeant on the phone. I began to wonder what effect it would have if I were to call out and tell them.

"Hey!" I shouted, but my voice was drowned out by a blast from the radio in the squad room. It died down immediately; someone must have hit a loud spot on the dial. I had an idea.

"Hey!" I shouted again, and again was drowned out. I opened the barred door and looked up and down the corridor. No one was in sight. Without making any unnecessary noise, but not stealthily, either, I walked as naturally as I could past the door to the squad room, where all heads were turned away, listening to the sensational pronouncements of Bill Bart, the radio gossip.

"… and in your commentator's view, this man is dangerous! After attacking a woman and setting fire to a restaurant, he was arrested and is being held for investigation, but I predict that the double-domes and alleged scientists will come up with some more gobbledegook and we ordinary citizens will be left in the dark as to why or how Graham is causing all this trouble. So far, fortunately, no one has been seriously injured, but I predict…."

I left and went on down the corridor.

So Bill Bart was giving me a play! What kind of crazy guesswork was he foisting on his public, I wondered, and came to the desk room. I looked in at the door. On one side, a sergeant was talking to an elderly worried-looking couple and never turned his head. On the other, a gray-haired lieutenant sitting at the raised desk dropped his glasses as I came in. They fell on the floor and smashed.

"Mother of God!" he muttered and gave me a cursory glance. "Good night, Doctor," he said. "Not that there's anything good about it." He was fumbling in the desk as I walked out of the door.

On the other side of the street, in the shadows, was a man who crossed over as I came down the steps. It was McGill.

"I had a hunch this might happen," he said, taking my arm. "The car's up ahead. Vinelli came here as quick as he could, but he slipped coming along the street and broke his ankle."

"Judas!" I said. "I *am* sorry! I feel responsible. Where are we going?"

He didn't answer me at first; he just kept hurrying me along. One of those New York siroccos[8] was pretending to cool the city, and at the corner I saw his old coupe with the parking lights on. A saloon next to us was closing up and a few late customers came out onto the sidewalk. One customer, on seeing me, stopped and turned to the others.

"That's the guy I was telling you about! That's Graham!"

I saw then that it was our telephone repairman from the afternoon. He looked reasonably sober, but his friends did not.

"Oh, yeah?" one of these said, eying me belligerently. "I thought we just heard Bill Bart broadcast the cops had him."

"Right," said another of them. "He's escaped! I'll hold him and you go on in and phone 'em."

"Nah, the joint's closed. Police station's right around the corner. I'll go tell 'em. Hold onto him now!"

The repairman and three of his pals began to advance warily and the other one ran down Charles Street, but at that moment we heard excited yapping

---

[8] hot wind

and a small dog chasing a cat came tearing up the street. The cat had a fish head in its mouth and, ignoring us, ran through the middle of the group, dropping the fish head. The dog followed almost instantly, only he ran between the repairman's legs, upsetting him. In falling, the repairman tripped his neighbor, who fell on him, and another one fell on top of them. The remaining one stepped on the fish head.

"Black cat!" he cried as he joined the others on the sidewalk. "Crossed my path!"

We got into McGill's car and he pulled away fast. As I looked back, the four men were flailing around, but they saw the direction we took. I also thought I saw the street lamp behind us go out.

"That was a lucky break!" I said. "I mean the cat and dog."

"Don't give it a thought," McGill said, driving fast but carefully up Hudson Street. "You're being watched over and protected. We're going up to my office and have a conference and we're going to drive like hell. I have an idea this thing may not be able to do much more than hang onto you. Maybe we can even shake it."

"Hang onto me?"

"Yes, you're the nucleus."

We were at the top of the ramp to the Westside Highway and he abruptly put on more speed; no traffic was in sight.

"But what is it?" I asked a little wildly. "How's it doing it? Why pick on me?"

"I don't know, but I'd say it picked you as the nucleus because you had just been the subject of various flukes—the taxi and subway and so on—so you represented a sample of what it's made of—flukes. I have a hunch you'll continue to be protected."

"Did you happen to catch Bill Bart's broadcast?"

"Yes, I did. On the car radio coming over. Not good. He said—"

In the rear-view mirror, I saw a police car overhauling us. We were doing a good sixty-five. "Here come the cops," I interrupted, but before McGill could answer, there was a faint pop and the police car wobbled and slowed to a stop, and was quickly out of sight.

"Blowout," I said.

"See what I mean?" McGill answered, and turned on two wheels into the 125th Street exit. Then he added, "Molly's waiting for us in my office."

I felt better.

We drove through some immortal gateway and McGill moderated his speed. He pulled up in front of a darkened building and we climbed the steps. It seemed cooler here and the wind was very strong. McGill tried the door, but it was locked. Then he felt in his pocket and swore.

"No key?" I asked.

He shook his head and then shook the door, and went through his pockets again. I reached forward and shook the door, too. The lock clicked and we went in. I made an apologetic gesture and McGill raised his eyebrows.

We climbed a flight of stairs, all dark except for a faint glow that came in from the campus lights, and then along an echoing hallway to an office in which were Molly and some unimportant items, among them a desk radio that she turned off as we came in.

She gave me her professional nurse's smile and I sat down next her. Molly's professional nurse's smile is not a phony "Everything's going to be all right," but a signal. It's supposed to mean "Never mind what these cretins are saying about you. You're okay."

I was a little puzzled that she showed no surprise to see me.

"Well," McGill said, "my hunch was right. He got out."

"So I see," said Molly, smiling at me proudly. "What happened? Knock over one of the jailers?"

I shook my head and told her, including the cat-and-dog episode and the police car blowout.

"Don't forget the lock downstairs," McGill said, and when I told her that, too, he added, "You see, I think it's beginning to take sides. I think it's watching out for its nucleus. Alec ought to be rather lucky right now."

"Well, I don't feel it," I said. "I feel hemmed in."

Molly glanced at me anxiously and turned back to him. "What do we do now?"

"First, before any more funny stuff happens, I want to rig up a few tests and see what's with Alec, if anything. I'll even test for EMF, Molly, just for the sake of satisfying you."

"For what?" I asked.

"Electromagnetic force. Come and give me a hand, Molly. Alec, you stay put and relax. We'll call you when we get set. I only hope to God the cops and the news hawks don't tumble to where we are."

They left and I went to the window and looked out at the wind blowing papers and dust into miniature tornadoes in the dim light, and wondered whether it was going to storm. A few belated students on the way to their dormitories evidently were wondering the same thing, for they were all looking up at the sky. I went to the desk and turned the radio on, low.

"… are doing all they can, which doesn't seem much," Bill Bart was saying breathlessly. "He was last seen speeding uptown on the Westshore Drive, but the cops lost him. The town is gripped in superstitious fear—it is now known that Graham was responsible for the elevators jamming in the I.T.V. Building this morning—but how did he do it? I ask you: how? And how has he turned off all the electric power in Greenwich Village? I contacted the power company for an explanation, but I was put off with the usual double talk. I say, and I repeat, *this man must be caught!* He is…."

I turned him off. So that was what the street light going off had meant.

In a little while, Molly came back. "All right, duck, come and be measured. He's got galvanometers and electronic devices and stuff, and he'll be able to detect anything you're emanating down to a milli-micro-whisker."

I followed her into the lab where I was sat down, taped up and surrounded with gadgets. McGill tried various things and read various dials. There were buzzing sounds and little lights blinked on and off, but at the end he shook his head.

"Nothing," he announced, "You're married to a non-ferrous, non-conducting, non-emanating, non-magnetic writer, Molly."

"He is, too!" she said. "He's as magnetic as the dickens."

"Possibly, but he isn't emanating anything. The damn thing apparently just likes him. As a nucleus, I mean."

"Is that bad?" Molly asked. "Could it be dangerous?"

"It's bad," I put in morosely.

"Also it could be good," McGill said, with a gleam of scientific enthusiasm, "Why, it wouldn't surprise me, Alec, if you could do anything you wanted to that involved chance."

I didn't like the guinea-pigs'-eye view of him I got, and told him so. "Except for a couple of minor escapes, it's been highly inconvenient," I said. "I don't want to seem ungrateful, but I wish it would go and help somebody else."

"But, my God, man! Do you realize if you went to the track tomorrow, your horse probably couldn't lose?"

"I wouldn't get that far," I grumbled.

"And I bet if somebody threw a knife at you, it would miss!" McGill went on, ignoring me. "Here, I'd like to try an experiment...."

"Now, hold on!" I said.

"*McGill!* Are you *crazy?*" Molly cried, but he ignored her also and opened his desk drawer, from which he took a pair of dice.

"Roll me some sevens, Alec," he said, handing them to me.

"I thought we came here for a conference," I protested. "And I don't know whether you know about it, but there's been a Village-wide electric power failure and I'm being blamed, according to Bill Bart."

"Holy cow! When did you hear that?"

"On your radio just now. Furthermore, he says the whole town is gripped in 'superstitious terror.'"

"That could be true," McGill answered. "Most people haven't progressed beyond the Dark Ages. Look what happened with Orson Welles' broadcast about the Martians."

"Maybe we ought to leave town for a while." Molly said. "We could go to Oyster Bay or somewhere." Then she glanced up. "What's that noise?"

Outside, I now noticed, mingled with the soughing of the wind, a susurrus of many voices. We went to the lab windows. A crowd of two or three hundred people was standing in the campus, staring up at the sky over us.

"What are they looking at?" McGill asked. "No one can possibly know we're here."

I started to lean out of the window, twisting up my head to see what it could be.

"Don't do that, Alec! They'll see you!" McGill warned, and I pulled my head in.

"Can we get on the roof?" I asked, but Molly suddenly said, "Look who's here." Three squad cars drove up and several policemen got out.

"Perhaps we ought to sort of very gently turn the lights off," I suggested.

Molly immediately snapped off the shaded bench lamp, which was all that was on in the lab. This left McGill's office light, and I started toward it.

"Hadn't we better run for it?" Molly said, but a loud banging on the front door downstairs answered her.

"I hope that damn lock doesn't give again!" McGill breathed.

"They'll break it down!" Molly gasped.

"Like hell. It's University property and they can't possibly have gotten a search warrant so quickly at this time of night."

• • •

Vocabulary words:

Find these words in the section, write the sentence they are used in, and write your own definition. If you are stuck, look it up in the dictionary, but still write a definition in your own words.

upsetting
cretins
emanating
soughing

Comprehension/extension questions:

What made the narrator decide to break out of jail?

Do you think there is a guiding hand toward all that is happening, or pure luck?

• • •

From outside came a loud voice: "Alec Graham! Are you in there?"

"Don't answer," said McGill. "And keep away from the windows. I guess they saw the light in my office." He leaned out. "What do you want?" he shouted.

"This is the police. Open up!"

"I won't unless you have a warrant!"

There was no more shouting. They seemed to be parlaying among themselves, but the crowd had a menacing sound. A brilliant light suddenly hit our windows, illuminating the lab ceiling—a police searchlight. I saw that Molly had disappeared and I assumed she had gone into McGill's office.

"These guys mean business," he said, "but what the hell brought them?"

"Something on the roof. That's what they're all looking at, so why don't we go up and see?"

"All right, but you'd better stay down here. There's no parapet and they'll see you."

He started for the door and I decided to follow—at least as far as the trapdoor, or whatever gave onto the roof—when Molly came in from the hall. She looked scared.

"My God! I climbed an iron ladder and took a look outside. There's a small cyclone over us—a ton of torn papers and dust and junk whirling around like a waterspout! They'd be able to see it for blocks!"

"Oh, great," McGill groaned. "Now it's playing tricks with the wind. That's how they spotted us."

"We've got to get out of here, McGill," said Molly.

"Maybe the best thing would be for me to give myself up to the cops," I said.

"I don't know whether they'd be able to get you through that mob," McGill replied. "Just listen to them. I only wish I could think of some way to satisfy the damn crystal or whatever it is. I have the feeling it wants something. It can't be merely fooling around for no reason. But there doesn't seem to be any motive beyond the fact that it's apparently on your side. How did it start? That's what I wish I knew."

He absently turned the bench lamp on again. I shrugged unhappily and scratched my cheek. In so doing, I pulled the piece of pink adhesive tape loose and it began to bleed again.

"Cut yourself shaving, darling?" Molly asked me.

"No," I said. "As a matter of fact, it was a kind of freak accident."

"Oh?" McGill lifted his head interestedly. "Anything involving you and a fluke I want to hear about. Tell Papa."

I did and McGill began to get his dedicated look. "You say this piece of glass just blew up? What did it look like? How big was it?"

"I only saw it for a second. It was dirty and I'd say about two feet across—more or less round and with flat places all over it."

McGill came toward me in a state of great excitement. "That piece that hit your cheek—did it merely nick you or is it embedded? If it *is* embedded...." He picked up a bottle of alcohol and a piece of cotton and took a lens out of a drawer. "Molly, there's a pair of tweezers in my desk. Will you fetch them?" He tilted the light up onto my face and dabbed the cut with the alcohol.

"Ouch!"

"Keep still. It'll sting a little.... Yes, I think I can see it." He took the tweezers from Molly, who had returned, and neatly removed something from the cut. He held it under the light and looked at it through the lens. Then he rinsed it under the water faucet, dried it on a piece of filter-paper and looked at it again. "Well, it looks like glass. I don't know. Maybe it's the nucleus of the glass chunk and...." His voice trailed off and he frowned at nothing in particular, putting the fragment down on the filter-paper.

I picked it up. It seemed like a bit of sand, only brighter.

McGill's concern over this new object of interest had been so intent that for a few minutes our attention was diverted, but now Molly began to pace up and down. There didn't seem to be anything for us to do, and unlike most nurses, waiting makes her nervous. She was looking at the display of various chemicals and reagents on the shelves.

"What's that stuff?" she asked, pointing to a large jar of black powder labeled Deflocculated Graphite. "I bet those cops have gone for a search warrant."

"Finely divided carbon," McGill said. "Damn, I wish I could think of something! A chunk of glass… blowing up…."

"Graphite is carbon?" Molly said. "You don't think they'd actually *do* anything to Alec, do you?"

"It's another form of carbon. A diamond is still another: the rare crystalline form," he said. "I wouldn't put it past that mob to do anything."

"Oh, yes. I remember that in chemistry," Molly said. "But the police wouldn't let them, McGill, would they?"

"I've got an idea—" I tried to break in.

"They might not be able to stop them," McGill replied.

"We've got to get *out* of here!" Molly said for the second time.

"If a diamond—" I began.

"With a helicopter, we might," McGill said. "Right now, we're surrounded."

"How about hiding Alec?" Molly asked. "You and I could act innocent."

"I don't *want* to be hidden," I objected. "My idea is—"

"Or better yet, we could act guilty. That would appeal to them, wouldn't it, McGill?"

"They'd tear the place apart if they got in," McGill said.

I took a surreptitious look out of the windows again. It seemed to hit me that our being surrounded was an exaggeration; most of the crowd was centered about the police car directly in front of the main door.

They had an ugly look, and while I didn't like the idea of being alone, neither did I relish the thought of my presence possibly causing my wife and my best friend to be the victims of mob violence, for although the police might, in the absence of a warrant, refrain from breaking in, the mob might not. So I decided to leave, confident that some bizarre manifestation would lead them away from the lab, and that no matter where I went, I could hardly be worse off. To keep moving was my best bet.

Molly and McGill were still discussing the situation as I tip-toed into the hall. There surely would be a back door—probably in the basement—and I went down three flights to a cement-floored corridor. Then, with lighted matches, I found my way to a door at the back of the building, at the end. I opened it and peered out, to see a retaining wall and stone steps leading up to ground level. I eased out into the areaway and pulled the door shut, noticing that I still held the folded filter-paper with the fragment in it. The lock clicked and I realized that my bridge was, as they say, burned behind me.

Two cops were talking together a little way to my right, but their backs were turned and they were looking up. I, too, looked and saw the whirlpool of debris, which was exactly as Molly had described and quite as attention-calling. Clutching the filter-paper like a talisman, I climbed the steps and gumshoed away to the left, but as I got to the corner, I met a group of young men, also looking up.

One of these was saying, "That's a lynch mob, if ever I saw one! I don't get it."

"Mob psychology, that's the answer," explained another.

My heart congealed, but they walked right by me. It suddenly occurred to me that any newspapers that had carried the story would scarcely have been able to dig up a photograph of me yet. All I had to do was to walk out of the campus, for who would recognize me? Where I would go then was something I could decide later.

So I started out with more assurance, but I took the precaution to act like an onlooker by glancing up over my shoulder now and then at the airborne maelstrom.

As I got to the other side of the open space, I had another shock. A few yards ahead was another group of policemen, one of whom, I saw with dismay, was the lieutenant from Charles Street, and he was beginning to turn around. I barely had time to duck into a doorway to avoid being seen. I had the feeling of a member of the I.R.A. in Dublin during the Troubles, and I crouched against the door.

I could now hear the lieutenant's voice: "Of course he's up there! Maddigan'll be here with a warrant any minute now and we'll...." His voice faded away.

Behind me, the door suddenly opened and I almost fell. A young student holding some notebooks emerged.

"Sorry," he said, and walked toward the crowd.

The door had not yet closed and I slipped in, with my heart irretrievably contracted to the size of a buckshot. I could just make out in the dim light that I was at the bottom of the fire stairs, so I climbed to the third floor and went into a classroom, then on into an office somewhat like McGill's, that faced toward the lab building.

From here, I had a perfect view of the crowd, the police, the upper facade of the labs, brightly lit by the searchlight and, over all, the spinning papers and dust, which even as I looked began to die down. I was unable to see Molly or McGill and wondered whether they had noticed my absence and were worrying.

I saw a phone on the desk at my side and considered calling up McGill's office, but first I wanted to think over my new idea. I pulled down the shades and turned on the reading lamp, by the light of which I re-examined the fragment I had been carrying around all day. It sparkled brilliantly. On the desk, beside an onyx pen-set, a golf trophy and a signed golf ball, was a leather-framed photograph of a blank-faced young woman holding a pudgy little boy. I picked it up and rubbed the glass with the tiny fragment. It left a faint but undeniable scratch. So I was right about one thing.

Then I called McGill's office. In a few moments, I heard the receiver lifted, but no voice. "This is the nucleus," I said, and I heard of sigh of relief from McGill.

"Where in hell are you?"

"Across the way. Look, out of your window and I'll turn my light off and on again." I did so.

"You're in Professor Crandal's office. Why did you leave?"

"We'll go into that later. McGill, that fragment is a diamond."

"What!"

"At any rate, it scratches glass."

"Why didn't you tell me that before? And where is it? I couldn't find it anywhere."

"I was sidetracked. I've got it here. Now my idea—"

"A diamond! I begin to see light. Give with the idea, Alec."

"Well, there was all this talk of crystals and then you were telling Molly about carbon and diamonds, and it occurred to me that what we have is something trying to crystallize—something that once *was* a crystal, and got broken up and wants to re-form. It keeps trying with playing cards and pigeons and automobiles, but it's no go. Why don't we give it some carbon to play with, McGill?"

• • •

Vocabulary words:

Find these words in the section, write the sentence they are used in, and write your own definition. If you are stuck, look it up in the dictionary, but still write a definition in your own words.

parlaying
surreptitious
congealed

Comprehension/extension questions:

What was he right about? What has he figured out about the fragment?

• • •

There was a short silence. I looked across at the office, but I couldn't see him. I noticed a piece of dirty newspaper that had fallen out of the maelstrom and had caught on a thick wire that stretched from one of the lab windows to immediately below mine—some kind of aerial, I imagined. Then I saw that the maelstrom, rather than breaking up, as I had thought, was moving over in my direction. I would be pointed out again.

"You mean the graphite, I suppose," McGill said. "Why in hell did you leave and take the fragment with you?"

"I forgot it was in my hand," I said, dodging the first part of the question. "Nobody on the campus recognized me, so I guess I can walk back." Then I remembered the locked basement door and the fact that I could scarcely be let in by McGill, with the cops standing around, but I was feeling light-headed and damage-proof. It was protecting its nucleus, which, even if I wasn't any more, I had in my hand. My crystalline rabbit's foot.

"Hold on a second," I said. "I've got another idea."

I put down the receiver, and picked up the golf ball from the desk, and put it on the floor. I stood up and put my right foot on it and, holding my breath, I raised my other foot. In any event, I would not have far to fall—but I did not fall. I remained upright, holding the filter-paper and wobbling a little. Then I relaxed and closed my eyes—still I did not fall. The rabbit's foot was working, just as McGill said. I stepped down two inches and picked up the phone.

"I'm coming across," I said. "That is, if the wire that runs over here from the lab is strong enough to hold me."

"Alec! You're nuts!" McGill said, and I hung up. (Diamonds of the world, unite! You have nothing to lose but your nucleus.)

I took a look over the sill at the wire. It was held by a powerful steel eye-bolt, securely attached to the brickwork. Clutching the diamond fragment in its paper, I climbed over the sill and put a foot on the wire and felt immediately seasick. The wire vibrated like a harpstring, but did not give noticeably, and I put my other foot on it. Then I almost blacked out and closed my eyes.

When I opened them again, I found I had progressed some distance into the void. Nothing was holding me from over-balancing, but my body seemed to right itself automatically, as if I were a veteran tightrope walker.

In a frozen daze, I edged along, keeping my eyes fixed on the distant window in which I could see McGill and Molly watching me with white faces.

When I was about half way, the crowd caught sight of me and yelled. A man with a broad-brimmed hat ran out from the others and, to my horror, pulled out a gun. Another man picked up a stone, wound himself up like a sand-lot pitcher, and hurled it just before the other pulled his trigger. They were excellent shots: the stone was hit by the bullet and both disintegrated. The man's gun jammed at his second try and the two heroes were grabbed by the police.

With my heart pounding, I kept going, until, about four yards from safety, my foot caught, and I looked down again. There was a splice in the wire, sticking up from which was a sharp end. I staggered and righted myself... and let go of the filter-paper.

By now, the maelstrom was directly over me and my talisman was caught in the updraft. It did not fall, but I did. After a sickening instant, I was brought up with a jerk that nearly strangled me. The back of my coat had caught on the projecting wire and I swung there like an unused marionette.

The crowd shouted and milled around, and the cops called out directions to each other. One order was to send for the Fire Department. I found I could breathe, but I could not look down.

The all-important paper was fluttering around near the lab window and McGill was making grabs at it. Then it suddenly blew right in by him. His head reappeared and he shook his clasped hands at me. Molly remained at the window, her eyes round, the fingers of each hand crossed. I essayed a debonair smile, which she tried to answer. In the distance, I heard the owl-sound of approaching fire engines.

From behind Molly there suddenly came an intense blue light, which rapidly increased until she became a dark silhouette, and I could just make out McGill looking at the glare, his eyes shielded by what I took to be a deep-blue bottle. His stance suggested elation. There appeared to be a terrific indrauft—all the window shades were blowing straight into the lab and Molly's red hair streamed behind her.

In what was actually almost no time, I heard the Fire Department turn into the campus, and one piece of equipment skidded to a stop directly under me. There was the sound of a winch and then I felt something touch my foot. At that moment, my jacket gave way with a tearing sound, Molly closed her eyes, and I landed like an oversize tarantula on top of the fireman's ladder.

Firemen and cops were climbing toward me, alternated like meat and tomatoes on a shish-kebab. First to reach me was my friend the lieutenant. He re-arrested me and pulled. I shook my head to his earnest entreaties and hung on with the tenacity of the unbrave. It seems to be impossible to detach a determined man from a ladder when you are also on it.

He and his friends gave up finally and ordered the ladder lowered, but one last fluke intervened—if it was a fluke. The machinery refused to work and we drove away, with me swaying grandly on my perch.

The lieutenant had the hook-and-ladder driven to a distant police station, where in due course Vinelli, the lawyer, arrived with his foot in a cast, and I was bailed out. The cops showed me surprising consideration; it turned out they were furious at the irresponsible riding they had been getting from Bill Bart. A scientific bigshot that McGill knew, named Joe Stein, convinced them I was in no way to blame, and the case was dropped. Professor Stein gave a wonderfully incomprehensible but tranquilizing statement to the press, and Molly and I went to Oyster Bay.

"In two weeks, everybody'll have forgotten all about it," the lieutenant told us. "You may even be a hero. I don't know."

Before we left, we went with McGill to the lab and saw the diamond. It sat on a bench, gleaming brilliant, smooth-faceted and without a flaw. It was at least two feet across, about the same as the chunk of "glass" on Fifty-first Street.

"The cops never recognized what it was," McGill said, "it being so big."

"Who would?" Molly asked. "McGill, I've got an idea—"

"All I had to do," McGill said, ignoring her, "was to put the graphite on some cinder blocks and the fragment on the graphite. Then I turned a bunsen flame on it and it caught fire with a terrifically bright flame— very small—I guess you saw it." I nodded. "It didn't give off any heat," he went on. "Adiabatic process. And it got its necessary pressure from the random motions together of the graphite particles. Some random motions! When that was used up, it started on the cinder blocks and then the CO_2 in the air. That's what caused the suction: the blinds were blown straight in. You probably missed that." I shook my head. "Anyway, this thing—"

"McGill," Molly interrupted, "I've got an *idea*!"

"—this thing has got to be dumped out at sea."

"Oh," Molly said, looking crestfallen. "I was just going to say why don't we break a piece off and sell it in Amsterdam?"

"Good God, no! That would only start it up all over again!"

"Just a *little* piece, McGill?"

"NO!"

With Stein's help, McGill convinced the police that the thing had to be dumped, and we dropped it off a police launch beyond Sandy Hook, to their bored perplexity. They would have been still more puzzled if they had known what it was.

McGill came down to Oyster Bay for the weekend and we played a game of gin rummy—a truly memorable game, because the cards behaved and I even lost a little.

He congratulated me in a preoccupied way, which annoyed me. "I should think you'd be gladder than that," I told him.

"I am," he said. "But there's something else—"

"What's that?" asked Molly, worried.

"The schools of fish are traveling head to tail. I'm wondering if that's just the beginning of another mess."

We went back to playing gin rummy, but our minds weren't on what we were doing. They haven't been since. Just yesterday, an ocean liner chased its berthing tugboats away and went sightseeing up the Hudson River.

• • •

Vocabulary words:
Find these words in the section, write the sentence they are used in, and write your own definition. If you are stuck, look it up in the dictionary, but still write a definition in your own words.

maelstrom
talisman
debonair

Comprehension/extension questions:

What did the narrator mean by "Diamonds of the world, unite!"

What would you have done with the diamond? Would you have used it? Destroyed it?

I am a Nucleus, by Stephen Barr, Published February 1957

Stephen Barr published several short works and a couple of essays in the late 1960s-70s, and a poem in 1925.

FRESH AIR FIEND

By KRIS NEVILLE

Illustrated by KARL ROGERS

Sick and helpless, he was very lucky to have a faithful native woman to nurse him. Or was he?

He rolled over to look at the plants. They were crinkled and dead and useless in the narrow flower box across the hut. He tried to draw his arm under his body to force himself erect. The reserve oxygen began to hiss in sleepily. He tried to signal Hertha to help him, but she was across the room with her back to him, her hands fumbling with a bowl of dark, syrupy medicine. His lips moved, but the words died in his throat.

He wanted to explain to her that scientists in huge laboratories with many helpers and millions of dollars had been unable to find a cure for liguna fever. He wanted to explain that no brown liquid, made like cake batter, would cure the disease that had decimated the crews of two expeditions to Sitari and somehow gotten back to cut down the population of Wiblanihaven.

But, watching her, he could understand what she thought she was doing. At one time she must have seen a pharmacist put chemicals into a mortar and grind them with a pestle. This, she must have remembered, was what people did to make medicine, and now she put what chemical-appearing substances she could locate—flour, powdered coffee, lemon extract, salt— into a bowl and mashed them together. She was very intent on her work and it probably made her feel almost helpful.

Finally she moved out of his field of vision; he found that he could not turn his head to follow her with his eyes. He lay conscious but inert, like waterlogged wood on a river bottom. He heard sounds of her movement. At last he slept.

He awakened with a start. His head was clearer than it had been for hours. He listened to the oxygen hissing in again. He tried to read the dial on the far wall, but it blurred before his eyes.

"Hertha," he said.

She came quickly to his cot.

"What does the oxygen register say?"

"Oxygen register?"

He gritted his teeth against the fever which began to shake his body mercilessly until he wanted to scream to make it stop. He became angry even as the fever shook him: angry not really at the doctors; not really at any one thing. Angry because the mountains did not care if he saw them; angry that the air did not care if he breathed it. Angry because, between planets, between suns, the coldness of space merely waited, not giving a damn.

Several years ago—ten, twenty, perhaps more—some doctor had finally isolated a strain of the filterable virus of liguna fever that could be used as a vaccine: too weak to kill, but strong enough to produce immunity against its more virulent brother strains. That opened up the Sitari System for colonization and exploration and meant that the men who got there first would make fortunes.

So he went to the base at Ke, first selling his strip mine property and disposing of his tools and equipping his spaceship for the intersolar trip; and at Ke they shot him full of the disease. But his bloodstream built no antibodies. The weakened virus settled in his nervous system and there was no way of getting it out. The doctors were very sorry for him, and they assured him it was a one-in-ten-thousand phenomenon. Thereafter, he suffered recurrent paralytic attacks.

If it had not been for the advance warning—a pain at the base of his spine, a moment of violent trembling in his knees—he would have been forced to give up solitary strip mining altogether. As it was, whenever he felt the warning, he had to hurry to the nearest colony and be hospitalized for the duration of the attack. He had had four such warnings on this satellite, and three times he had gone to Pastiville on Helio and been cared for and come away with less money than he had gone with.

His bank credit, once large, had slowly dribbled away, and now he made just about enough from his mining to care for himself during illness. He could not afford to hunt for less dangerous, less isolated work. It would not pay enough, for he knew how to do very little that civilization needed done. He was finally trapped; no longer could he afford a pilot for the long flight from Helio to a newer frontier, and he could not risk the trip alone.

He lay waiting for the new spasm of fever and stared at Hertha who, this time, would care for him here and he would not need to go to a hospital. Perhaps, after a little while, he would be able to save enough to push on, through the awful indifference of space, to some new world where, with luck, there would be a sudden fortune.

Then he could go back to civilization.

He realized bitterly that he was merely telling himself he would go back. He knew there was only one direction he could go, and that direction was not back.

Hertha waited, hurt-eyed, moving her pudgy hands helplessly.

When the shaking subsided, he explained through chattering teeth about the oxygen register across the room, and she went away.

• • •

Vocabulary words:
Find these words in the section, write the sentence they are used in, and write your own definition. If you are stuck, look it up in the dictionary, but still write a definition in your own words.

mortar
virulent

Comprehension/extension questions:

What does the narrator think of Hertha? Why?

• • •

The fever vanished completely, leaving him listless. His hand, lying on the rough blanket, was abnormally white. He wiggled the fingers, but he could not feel the wool.

His mouth was dry and he wanted a drink of water.

Hertha moved out of his range of vision. He shifted his head on the damp pillow and watched her out of the corner of his eye.

He had never heard her real name, but she did not seem to object to his name for her.

> I am that which began;
> Out of me the years roll;
> Out of me God and man;
> I am equal and whole;
> God changes, and man,
> And the form of them bodily;
> I am the soul.

He tried to sit up again, but he was very weak. He wanted to quote it to her and tell her what he had never told her: that the name of it was *Hertha* and that it had been written long ago by a man named Swinburne, and he wanted to explain why he had named her after a poem, because it was very funny.

The harsh light hurt his eyes and made him feel dizzy. He lay watching her as she bent toward the oxygen dial, wrinkling her face in animal concentration, trying to read it for him. Her puzzled expression was pathetic; it reminded him of the first time he had seen her.

The walls began to spin crazily, for the hut had been intended for only one person.

He remembered the first time he saw her, cowering in a filthy alleyway in the Miramus. At first he thought she had taken some food from a garbage pail and was trying to conceal it by holding it to her breast. But when the flare of a rocket leaving the field two blocks away lit the area for a moment, he saw that she was holding a tiny welikin, terribly mangled, looking as if it had just been run over by a heavy transport truck. He took it away from her and threw it into the darkness, shuddering.

"It was dead," he said.

She continued to stare at him, starting to cry silently, big, round, salt tears that she brushed at with reddened hands.

"My—my—" she stammered.

He had an eerie feeling that she was trying to say, "My baby," and he felt a little chill of pity creep up his spine.

"What do you do?" he asked kindly.

"Sweep floors. I work a little for the Commander's wife. Around her home."

"How did you get here?"

Still crying, she said, "On a rocket."

"Of course. What I meant was…." But he did not need to ask how she had gotten passed the emigration officers. Some influential man—such things could happen, especially when the destination was a relatively new frontier, such as Helio, where there was little danger of investigation—had seen to it that certain answers were falsified; and a little money and a corrupt official had conspired to produce a passport which read, "Mentally and physically fit for colonization."

The influential man had, in effect, bought and paid for a personal slave to bring with him to the stars. She would not know of her legal rights. She would be easily frightened and confused. And then something had happened, and for some reason she had been abandoned to shift for herself. Perhaps she had run away.

He looked away from her face. This was none of his affair.

"Never mind," he said. He reached into his pocket and gave her a few coins and then turned and walked rapidly away, suddenly anxious to see the bright, remembered face of the young colonist, Doris, Don's friend; a face that would chase away the memory of this pathetic creature.

After a moment, he heard the pad of her feet hopefully, fearfully following him.

She was standing beside his cot again, and he concentrated to make the walls stop spinning.

"It had a blue line."

"Yes, I know. Where?"

She showed him with her fingers. "This much."

"Halfway up?" he prompted.

Dumbly, she nodded.

He looked at the plants. "Hertha, listen. I've got to talk before the paralysis comes back. You'll have to listen very carefully and try to understand. I'll be all right in about ten days. You know that?"

She nodded again.

He took a deep breath that seemed to catch in his throat. "But you'll have to go outside before then."

Hertha whimpered and fluttered her hands nervously.

"I know you're afraid," he said. "I wouldn't ask you, but it has to be done. I can't go. You can see that, can't you? It has to be done."

"Afraid!"

"Nonsense!" he said harshly. "There's nothing to be afraid of. Put on the outside suit and nothing can hurt you."

Moaning in fear, she shook her head.

"Listen, Hertha! You've *got* to do it. For *me*!" He did not like to make the appeal personal. He would have preferred to convince her that fear of the outside was groundless. It was not possible. He had attempted, again and again, to explain that the tiny satellite with its poison air was completely harmless as long as she wore a surface suit. There was no alien life, no possible danger, outside this tiny square of insulated hut and breathable air. But it was useless. And the personal appeal was the only course remaining. It was as much for her sake as his; she also needed oxygen, but she could never understand that fact.

"For you?" she asked.

He nodded, feeling the fever rise. His face twisted in pain, and he stared pleadingly into her cow-like eyes: dumb eyes, animal eyes, brown and trusting and... loyal. The paralysis struck. His voice would not come up out of his chest and the dizziness swamped his mind, and, in fever, he was once again in Pastiville, the nearest planet with an oxygen atmosphere.

Hertha followed him up the alley, out into the cheap glitter of Windopole Avenue, a rutted, smelly street which was the center of the port-workers' section. She followed him across Windopole, up Venus, across Nineshime. He turned into the Lexo Building, which had become shabby since he had seen it last, when it had been freshly painted. She did not follow him inside, and he breathed a sigh of relief and tried to put her out of his mind as he walked up the stairs to the room 17B.

After a moment's hesitation, his heart knocking with pleasant anticipation, he pressed the buzzer.

"Come in."

He found the knob, twisted open the door, entered.

"Why Jimmy!" the girl said in what seemed to be surprise and heavy delight. She crossed to him quickly and offered her lips to be kissed. "It's good to see you!"

He took half a step backward, trying to keep the shock out of his face.

"Oh, it's *so* good to see you, Jimmy! Sit down. Tell me all about it, about everything. Did you make loads and loads of money? When did you get back? How's the lig fever?"

He sat down, scarcely listening, studying the apartment, feeling vaguely ill. She was chattering, he realized, to overcome her embarrassment.

"The books you ordered came. I've got them right here. They're all there but some poetry or other. There was a letter about that, but the people just said they didn't have it in stock. I opened it to see if it required an answer. Just a sec. I'll get them for you." She left the room with quick, nervous strides.

The apartment had been redone since he had seen it. There were now expensive drapes at the windows, imported from somewhere; a genuine Earth tapestry hung above the door. Plump silken pillows scattered on the floor and a late model phono-general in the corner, with a gleaming cabinet and record spool accessory box.

She came back with the books, neatly done up in a bundle.

"I guess you still read as much as ever? Don said you always were a great reader."

Uncomfortably, he stood up.

She put the books on a low serving table, moistened her lips to make them glistening red. "Sit *down*, Jimmy!"

He still stood.

"*Jimmy!*" she said in mock anger. "Sit down! Goodness, it's good to have a fellow Earthman to talk to. I was so busy when you came by the other time, we scarcely had a *minute* to talk. I'd just got here, you remember.... Well, I'm settled now, so we'll just have to have a nice, long talk."

He shifted on his feet.

"I don't suppose you've heard from Don?" Her voice was strained, almost desperate. "Isn't it the oddest thing, him knowing you and me, and both of us right here?"

"He told me to write how you were getting along?"

"… Oh."

He smiled without humor and felt like an old man. He wanted to explain how he had looked forward to seeing a person from his own planet again. Now he wanted to remind her of the girl he remembered: When she had just arrived, still unpacking, eager to start as a junior secretary for the League.

"Thank you for letting me send the books here," he said. The sickness was heavy in the pit of his stomach, and suddenly he was hard and bitter. He quoted softly:

> "The world forsaken,
> And out of mind
> Honor and labor,
> We shall not find
> The stars unkind."

"Old poetry? I guess you really do read a—" Then understanding made her eyes wince. "That wasn't intended to be very complimentary, was it, Jimmy?"

Her name was no longer Doris; it was any of a thousand, and her perfume, heavy in his nostrils, was not her perfume or any individual's. She was there before him; she was real. But along with her were a thousand names and a thousand scents. There was the painful nostalgia of recognizing a strange room.

Awkwardly he said, "I really must go. I'd like to have a long talk, but—"

Her lips parting in sudden artificiality, she crossed to him, reached for his hand with her own.

In his mind was the heavy futility of repeating the same thing senselessly until it lost all meaning.

"I apologize about the poem," he said, because he knew that it was not his place to speak of it.

"That's all right," she said with hollow cheerfulness. Her mouth jerked and her eyes darkened. "Please don't go yet."

The palms of his hands were moist. He looked around the apartment again, and he did not want to ask, to bring it out in cruel words. It was not the sort of thing one asked.

"I really must go," he repeated levelly.

She put her hands on his shoulders. "Please...."

And then he saw that she intended to bribe him in the only way she knew how, and he said, "Don't worry, I won't tell Don."

He saw relief on her face, and then he was out of the apartment, shaken. He felt as if he had been kicked in the stomach, and he was sickened and his hand trembled. He wanted to talk to someone and try to explain it.

Hertha was waiting when he came out to the street.

The fever passed; control of his body returned.

"For you?" Hertha asked.

He half propped himself up on the cot. He waved his hand weakly. "Those dead plants. You must throw them out and bring in more."

He listened tensely, imagining that he could hear the precious oxygen hiss in from the emergency tank to freshen and revitalize the dead air. Halfway down on the dial. Not enough for ten days, even for one person, unless the air was replenished by bringing in plants.

"Hertha, we've got to purify this air. Now listen. Listen carefully, Hertha. You've seen me dig up those plants on the outside?"

"Yes, I watch when you go out. I always watch, Jimmy."

"Good. You've got to do the same thing. You've got to go out and dig up some plants. You've got to bring them in here and plant them the way I did. You know which ones they are?"

"Yes," she said.

He closed his eyes, trying to think of a way to make her see how vital a thing a tiny plant could be. The complex chemistry of it bubbled to the surface of his mind. He wanted to tell her why the plants died in the artificial human atmosphere and had to be replaced every week or so. He wanted to tell her, but he was growing weaker.

"They purify the air by releasing oxygen. You understand?"

She nodded her head dumbly.

"You must bring in a great many plants, Hertha. Remember that—a *great* many. Don't forget that. When you go outside, through the locks, we lose air. Air is very precious, so you must bring in a great many plants."

"Yes, Jimmy."

"And you must plant them as I did."

"Yes, Jimmy."

He began to talk faster, in a race with the growing fever.

"I've gathered most of the oxygenating plants around the hut. So you may have to go into the forest to get enough."

"The—the forest?"

"You *must*, Hertha! You *must*!"

Her mouth twisted as if she were ready to cry. "For you. Yes, for you I will go into the forest."

The fever came back. His mind wandered away.

• • •

Vocabulary words:
Find these words in the section, write the sentence they are used in, and write your own definition. If you are stuck, look it up in the dictionary, but still write a definition in your own words.

pathetic
satellite
artificiality

Comprehension/extension questions:

Why are Jimmy and Doris so awkward?

Why do they need plants brought into the hut?

• • •

He was walking in the open air. He walked from Nineshime to Venus, down Venus to Windopole, up Windopole to "The Grand Eagle and Barrel." He went

246

in. Hertha came with him and sat down by his side at the bar.

The bartender looked at him oddly. "She with you, Mac?"

He turned to look at her; her dumb, brown eyes met his. He wanted to snarl: "Get the hell away! Leave me alone!" But he choked back the words. It was not Hertha he was angry with. She had done him no injury. She had merely followed him, perhaps because she knew of nothing else to do; perhaps because of temporary gratitude for the coins; perhaps in hope that he would buy her a drink. When the anger passed, he felt sorry for her again.

He said, "Want a drink?"

She shook her head without changing expression.

He looked at her and shrugged and thought that after a while she would get tired and go away. He ordered, and the bartender brought a bottle and one glass.

Hertha continued to stare at him; he tried to ignore her.

He drank. He thought it would get easier to ignore her as the level of the bottle fell. It didn't. He drank some more. It grew late.

"I gotta explain," he said, the liquor swirling in his mind.

She waited, cow-eyed.

"Ernest Dowson. Man's name. He wrote a poem— *Beata Solitudo*. I wanna explain this. Man lived long, long, long, long time ago. You listenin'? Okay. That's good. That's fine. He said—it's ver' importan' you should unnerstan' this—he said how you put honor and labor out of your mind when you... You're out here. What he meant, it's... It's... you see.... Now I gotta make you see all this. So you listen real close while I tell it to you. There was a man named...."

He wanted to explain how the frontier does things to people. He wanted to explain how society is a tight little box that keeps everything locked up and hidden, but how society breaks down and becomes fluid in the stars, and how people explode and forget what they learned in civilization, and how everything is unstable.

"This man, his name's—" he said.

He wanted to explain how the harsh elements and brute nature and space, the God-awful emptiness and indifference and the sense of aloneness and selfishness and....

There were a thousand things he wanted to tell her. They were all the things he had thought about as he followed the frontier. If he could get it all down right, he could make her see why he had to follow the frontier as long as there was anything left inside of him.

Maybe the rest of the people out here were that way, too. Maybe he had seen it in Doris' eyes tonight. Maybe that was why society broke down in the stars and civilization came only when men and women like him were gone.

He did not want to know how the rest felt. He did not know whether it would be more terrifying to learn that he was alone, or that he was not alone.

But just for tonight, he could tell the alien creature beside him. It would be safe to tell her—if the idea had not rusted inside of him so long that there were no longer any words to fit it.

But first he had to make her see his home planet and the great cities and the landscaped valleys and the majestic mountains and the people. He had to make her see the vast sweep of the explorers who first carried the race to a million planets, who devised faster-than-light ships and metals to make the ships out of, metals to hold their forms in the crucible beyond normal space. He had to make her see the colonists who tied all the world together with spans of steel commerce and then moved on in ever-widening circles. He wanted to give her the whole picture.

Then he wanted to explain the surge, the restlessness of the men at the frontier. Different men, he thought; from the womb of civilization, but unlike their brothers. The men who pushed out and out. Searching, always searching. He was afraid to find out if their reasons were the same as his. For himself, he had seen a thousand planets and a thousand new life-forms. But it was not enough. There were the vast, blank, empty, indifferent reaches of space beyond him, and that was what drove him on.

This he wanted to say to Hertha: No matter how far you go, the thing that gets you is that there's nothing that cares; no matter how far, the thing is that nothing cares; the thing is that nothing cares. It gets you. And you have to go on because some day, somewhere, there may be—something.

But he lost the trend of his thoughts completely, and he had another drink.

"Decent people come out here...."
What was he going to say about decent people?
"Stupid!" he cried, slapping her in the face.
She rubbed her cheek. "Stupid?"
He wanted to cry, for he had not known that he was brutal. "Can't you see?" he screamed, and it was necessary to explain it to her; and then it was not necessary. "You're like the awful, indifferent, mindless blackness of space, unreasoning!"
"Unreasoning," she repeated carefully.
"You're *Hertha*!"
"I'm Hertha," she said.

The period of calmness that returned after the fever was crystal and lucid, preceding, he knew, a severe, prolonged seizure.
"I'm afraid," she told him, shivering, "but I will go."
He watched her get into the light surface suit, clamp down the helmet with trembling hands. He was shaking with nervousness as she hesitated at the lock. Then she pulled it open. It clicked behind her. He heard the brief hiss of the oxygen replacing the air that had whooshed out.
And he felt sorry for her, alone, terrified, on the scaly, hard surface of the tiny satellite. He closed his eyes, pictured her walking past his strip mine, past the gleaming heap of minerals ready for the transport.
He felt tears in his eyes and yet he could not entirely explain his feelings toward her—half fear, sometimes half affection. But more important than that:

Why was she with him? What were her feelings? Had some sense of gratitude made her come? Affection?

He could not understand her. At times she seemed beyond all understanding. Her responses were mindless, almost mechanical, and that frightened him.

He remembered her dumb, apologetic caresses and her pathetically clumsy tenderness—or reflex; he could never be sure—and her eager yet reluctant hands and the always slightly hurt, slightly accusing look in her eyes, as if at every instant she was ready for a stinging blow, and her great sighs, muted as if fearing to be heard and….

He was drunk, screaming meaninglessly, and the bartender threw him out. The pavement cut his face. When he awoke, it was morning and he was in a strange room and she was in bed beside him.

She said, "I am Hertha. I brought you home. I will go with you."

The paralysis set in. He could not move. The tears froze on his cheeks, and he lay inert, thinking of her almost mindlessly fighting for his life in the alien outside.

Then she was back in the hut. So soon?

She looked at him, smiled through the transparent helmet at him. He could hear the precious oxygen hiss in to compensate for the air that had been lost when she entered.

He could see her eyes. They were proud. Relieved, too, as if she had been afraid he would be gone when she returned. He felt she had hurried back to be sure that he was still there.

She knelt by the flower bed and, without removing her suit, she held up the plant proudly. He could see the hard-packed dirt in the roots. Fascinated, he watched her scrape a planting hole. He watched her set the plant delicately and pat the soil with care.

Then she stood up.

He tried to move, to cry out. He could not.

He watched her until she went out of the range of his fixed eyes. She was going to the airlock again.

After a moment he heard the familiar hiss of oxygen.

She was going to get a great number of plants.

But one at a time.

• • •

Vocabulary words:
Find these words in the section, write the sentence they are used in, and write your own definition. If you are stuck, look it up in the dictionary, but still write a definition in your own words.

brute
frontier

Comprehension/extension questions:

What did Hertha do wrong?

Fresh Air Fiend, by Kris Neville, Published February 1952

Kris Neville was Born in Carthage, Missouri in May 9, 1915 and died December 23, 2980. He also used the names Henderson Starke and Kris Melville. Kris Neville published many short works in the 1950s and his works continue to be published in anthologies and chapbooks. He published four novels in the 1960s-70s.

CITIZEN JELL

By MICHAEL SHAARA
Illustrated by DICK FRANCIS

The problem with working wonders
is they must be worked—even when
they're against all common sense!

None of his neighbors knew Mr. Jell's great problem. None of his neighbors, in truth, knew Mr. Jell at all. He was only an odd old man who lived alone in a little house on the riverbank. He had the usual little mail box, marked "E. Jell," set on a post in front of his house, but he never got any mail, and it was not long before people began wondering where he got the money he lived on.

Not that he lived well, certainly; all he ever seemed to do was just fish, or just sit on the riverbank watching the sky, telling tall stories to small children. And none of that took any money to do.

But still, he *was* a little odd; people sensed that. The stories he told all his young friends, for instance—wild,

254

weird tales about spacemen and other planets—people hardly expected tales like that from such an old man. Tales about cowboys and Indians they might have understood, but spaceships?

So he was definitely an odd old man, but just how odd, of course, no one ever really knew. The stories he told the children, stories about space travel, about weird creatures far off in the Galaxy—those stories were all true.

Mr. Jell was, in fact, a retired spaceman.

Now that was part of Mr. Jell's problem, but it was not all of it. He had very good reasons for not telling anybody the truth about himself—no one except the children—and he had even more excellent reasons for not letting his own people know where he was.

The race from which Mr. Jell had sprung did not allow this sort of thing—retirement to Earth. They were a fine, tolerant, extremely advanced people, and they had learned long ago to leave undeveloped races, like the one on Earth, alone. Bitter experience had taught them that more harm than good came out of giving scientific advances to backward races, and often just the knowledge of their existence caused trouble among primitive peoples.

No, Mr. Jell's race had for a long while quietly avoided contact with planets like Earth, and if they had known Mr. Jell had violated the law, they would have come swiftly and taken him away—a thing Mr. Jell would have died rather than let happen.

Mr. Jell was unhuman, yes, but other than that he was a very gentle, usual old man. He had been born and raised on a planet so overpopulated that it was one vast city from pole to pole. It was the kind of place where a man could walk under the open sky only on rooftops, where vacant lots were a mark of incredible wealth. Mr. Jell had passed most of his long life under unbelievably cramped and crowded conditions—either in small spaceships or in the tiny rooms of unending apartment buildings.

When Mr. Jell had happened across Earth on a long voyage some years ago, he had recognized it instantly as the place of his dreams. He had had to plan very carefully, but when the time came for his retirement, he was able to slip away. The language of Earth was already on record; he had no trouble learning it, no trouble buying a small cottage on the river in a lovely warm place called Florida. He settled down quietly, a retired old man of one hundred and eighty-five, looking forward to the best days of his life.

And Earth turned out to be more wonderful than his dreams. He discovered almost immediately that he had a great natural aptitude for fishing, and though the hunting instinct had been nearly bred out of him and he could no longer summon up the will to kill, still he could walk in the open woods and marvel at the room, the incredible open, wide, and unoccupied room, live animals in a real forest, and the sky above, clouds seen through the trees—*real trees*, which Mr. Jell had seldom seen before. And, for a long while, Mr. Jell was certainly the happiest man on Earth.

He would arise, very early, to watch the sun rise. After that, he might fish, depending on the weather, or sit home just listening to the lovely rain on the roof, watching the mighty clouds, the lightning. Later in the afternoon, he might go for a walk along the riverbank, waiting for school to be out so he could pass some time with the children.

Whatever else he did, he would certainly go looking for the children.

A lifetime of too much company had pushed the need for companionship pretty well out of him, but then he had always loved children, and they made his life on the river complete. They *believed* him; he could tell them his memories in safety, and there was something very special in that, to have secrets with friends. One or two of them, the most trustworthy, he even allowed to see the Box.

• • •

Vocabulary words:
Find these words in the section, write the sentence they are used in, and write your own definition. If you are stuck, look it up in the dictionary, but still write a definition in your own words.

primitive
companionship
Comprehension/extension questions:

Why did Jell hide from his own people? Why wasn't he supposed to associate with earth men?

• • •

Now the Box *was* something extraordinary, even to so advanced a man as Mr. Jell. It was a device which analyzed matter, made a record of it, and then duplicated it. The Box could duplicate anything.

What Mr. Jell would do, for example, would be to put a loaf of bread into the Box, and press a button, and presto, there would be *two* loaves of bread, each perfectly alike, atom for atom. It would be absolutely impossible for anyone to tell them apart. This was the way Mr. Jell made most of his food, and all of his money. Once he had gotten one original dollar bill, the Box went on duplicating it—and bread, meat, potatoes, anything else Mr. Jell desired was instantly available at the touch of a button.

Once the Box duplicated a thing, anything, it was no longer necessary to have the original. The Box filed a record in its electronic memory, describing, say, bread, and Mr. Jell had only to dial a number any time he wanted bread. And the Box needed no fuel except dirt, leaves, old pieces of wood, just anything made out of atoms—most of which it would arrange into bread or meat or whatever Mr. Jell wanted, and the rest of which it would use as a source of power.

So the Box made Mr. Jell entirely independent, but it did even more than that; it had one other remarkable feature. It could be used also as a transmitter and receiver. Of matter. It was, in effect, the Sears Roebuck catalog of Mr. Jell's people, with its own built-in delivery service.

If there was an item Mr. Jell needed, any item at all, and that item was available on any of the planets ruled by Mr. Jell's people, Mr. Jell could dial for it, and it would appear in the Box in a matter of seconds.

The makers of the Box prided themselves on the speed of their delivery, the ease with which they could transmit matter instantaneously across light-years of space. Mr. Jell admired this property, too, but he could make no use of it. For once he had dialed, he would also be billed. And of course his Box would be traced to Earth. That Mr. Jell could not allow.

No, he would make do with whatever was available on Earth. He had to get along without the catalog.

And he really never needed the catalog, not at least for the first year, which was perhaps the finest year of his life. He lived in perfect freedom, ever-continuing joy, on the riverbank, and made some special friends: one Charlie, aged five, one Linda, aged four, one Sam, aged six. He spent a great deal of his time with these friends, and their parents approved of him happily as a free baby-sitter, and he was well into his second year on Earth when the first temptation arose.

Bugs.

Try as he might, Mr. Jell could not learn to get along with bugs. His air-conditioned, antiseptic, neat and odorless existence back home had been an irritation, yes, but he had never in his life learned to live with bugs of any kind, and he was too old to start now. But he had picked an unfortunate spot. The state of Florida was a heaven for Mr. Jell, but it was also a heaven for bugs.

There is probably nowhere on Earth with a greater variety of insects, large and small, winged and stinging, than Florida, and the natural portion of all kinds found their ways into Mr. Jell's peaceful existence. He was unable even to clear out his own house—never mind the endless swarms of mosquitoes that haunted the riverbank—and the bugs gave him some very nasty moments. And the temptation was that he alone, of all people on Earth, could have exterminated the bugs at will.

One of the best-selling export gadgets on Mr. Jell's home world was a small, flying, burrowing, electronic device which had been built specifically to destroy bugs on planets they traded with. Mr. Jell was something of a technician, and he might not even have had to order a Destroyer through the catalog, but there were other problems.

Mr. Jell's people had not been merely capricious when they formed their policy of non-intervention. Mr. Jell's bug-destroyer would kill all the bugs, but it would undoubtedly ruin the biological balance upon which the country's animal life rested. The birds which fed on the bugs would die, and the animals which fed on the birds, and so on, down a course which could only be disastrous. And even one of the little Destroyers would put an extraordinary dent in the bug population of the area; once sent out into the woods, it could not be recalled or turned off, and it would run for years.

No, Mr. Jell made the valiant decision to endure little itchy bumps on his arms for the rest of his days.

Yet that was only the first temptation. Soon there were others, much bigger and more serious. Mr. Jell had never considered this problem at all, but he began to realize at last that his people had been more right than he knew. He was in the uncomfortable position of a man who can do almost anything, and does not dare do it. A miracle man who must hide his miracles.

The second temptation was rain. In the middle of Mr. Jell's second year, a drought began, a drought which covered all of Florida. He sat by helplessly, day after day, while the water level fell in his own beloved river, and fish died gasping breaths, trapped in little pockets upstream. Several months of that produced Mr. Jell's second great temptation. Lakes and wells were dry all over the country, farms and orange groves were dry, there were great fires in the woods, birds and animals died by the thousands.

All that while, of course, Mr. Jell could easily have made it rain. Another simple matter, although this time he would have had to send away for the materials, through the Box. But he couldn't do that. If he did, *they* would come for him, and he consoled himself by arguing that he had no right to make it rain. That was not strictly controllable, either. It might rain and rain for several days, once started, filling up the lakes, yes, and robbing water from somewhere else, and then what would happen when the normal rainy season came?

Mr. Jell shuddered to think that he might be the cause, for all his good intentions, of vast floods, and he resisted the second temptation. But that was relatively easy. The third temptation turned out to be infinitely harder.

Little Charlie, aged five, owned a dog, a grave, sober, studious dog named Oscar. On a morning near the end of Mr. Jell's second year, Oscar was run over by a truck. And Charlie gathered the dog up, all crumpled and bleeding and already dead, and carried him tearfully but faithfully off to Mr. Jell, who could fix *anything*.

And Mr. Jell could certainly have fixed Oscar. Hoping to guard against just such an accident, he had already made a "recording" of Oscar several months before. The Box had scanned Oscar and discovered exactly how he was made—for the Box, as has been said, could duplicate anything—and Mr. Jell had only to dial Oscar number to produce a new Oscar. A live Oscar, grave and sober, atom for atom identical with the Oscar that was dead.

• • •

Vocabulary words:
Find these words in the section, write the sentence they are used in, and write your own definition. If you are stuck, look it up in the dictionary, but still write a definition in your own words.

instantaneously
capricious
valiant
Comprehension/extension questions:

What would be the consequences of exterminating all of the bugs in the world?

Does Mr. Jell's box remind you of another story in this book? What do you suppose is the moral of the story?

• • •

But young Charlie's parents, who had been unable to comfort the boy, came to Mr. Jell's house with him. And Mr. Jell had to stand there, red-faced and very sad, and deny to Charlie that there was anything he could do, and watch the look in Charlie's eyes turn into black betrayal. And when the boy ran off crying, Mr. Jell had the worst temptation of all.

He thought so at the time, but he could not know that the dog had not been the worst. The worst was yet to come.

He resisted a great many temptations after that, but now for the first time doubt had begun to seep in to his otherwise magnificent existence. He swore to himself that he could never give this life up. Here on the riverbank, dry and buggy as it well was, was still the most wonderful life he had ever known, infinitely preferable to the drab crowds he would face at home. He was an old man, grimly aware of the passage of time. He would consider himself the luckiest of men to be allowed to die and be buried here.

But the temptations went on.

First there was the Red Tide, a fish-killing disease which often sweeps Florida's coast, murdering fish by the hundreds of millions. He could have cured that, but he would have had to send off for the chemicals.

Next there was an infestation of the Mediterranean fruit fly, a bug which threatened most of Florida's citrus crop and very nearly ruined little Linda's father, a farmer. There was a Destroyer available which could be set to kill just one type of bug, Mr. Jell knew, but he would have had to order it, again, from the catalog. So he had to let Linda's father lose most of his life's savings.

Shortly after that, he found himself tempted by a young, gloomy couple, a Mr. and Mrs. Ridge, whom he visited one day looking for their young son, and found himself in the midst of a morbid quarrel. Mr. Ridge's incredible point of view was that this was too terrible a world to bring children into. Mr. Jell found himself on the verge of saying that he himself had personally visited forty-seven other worlds, and not one could hold a candle to this one.

He resisted that, at last, but it was surprising how close he had come to talking, even over such a relatively small thing as that, and he had concluded that he was beginning to wear under the strain, when there came the day of the last temptation.

Linda, the four-year-old, came down with a sickness. Mr. Jell learned with a shock that everyone on Earth believed her incurable.

He had no choice then. He knew that from the moment he heard of the illness, and he wondered why he had never until that moment anticipated this. There was, of course, nothing else he could do, much as he loved this Earth, and much as he knew little Linda would certainly have died in the natural order of things. All of that made no difference; it had finally come home to him that if a man is able to help his neighbors and does not, then he ends up something less than a man.

He went out on the riverbank and thought about it all that afternoon, but he was only delaying the decision. He knew he could not go on living here or anywhere with the knowledge of the one small grave for which he would be forever responsible. He knew Linda would not begrudge him those few moments, that one afternoon more. He waited, watching the sun go down, and then he went back into the house and looked through the catalog. He found the number of the serum and dialed for it.

The serum appeared within less than a minute. He took it out of the Box and stared at it, the thought of the life it would bring to Linda driving all despair out of his mind. It was a universal serum; it would protect her from all disease for the rest of her life. *They* would be coming for him soon, but he knew it would take them a while to get here, perhaps even a full day. He did not bother to run. He was much too old to run and hide.

He sat for a while thinking of how to get the serum to her, but that was no problem. Her parents would give her anything she asked now, and he made up some candy, injecting the serum microscopically into the chunks of chocolate, and then suddenly had a wondrous idea. He put the chunks into the Box and went on duplicating candy until he had several boxes.

When he was finished with that, he went visiting all the houses of all the good people he knew, leaving candy for them and their children. He knew he should not do that, but, he thought, it couldn't really do much harm, could it? Just those few lives altered, out of an entire world?

But the idea had started wheels turning in his mind, and toward the end of that night, he began to chuckle with delight. Might as well be flashed for a rogg as a zilb.

He ordered out one special little bug Destroyer, from the Box, set to kill just one bug, the medfly, and sent it happily down the road toward Linda's farm. After that, he duplicated Oscar and sent the dog yelping homeward with a note on his collar. When he was done with that, he ordered a batch of chemicals, several tons of it, and ordered a conveyor to carry it down and dump it into the river, where it would be washed out to sea and so end the Red Tide.

By the time that was over, he was very tired; he had been up the whole night. He did not know what to do about young Mr. Ridge, the one who did not want children. He decided that if the man was that foolish, nothing could help him. But there was one other thing he could do. Praying silently that once he started this thing, it would not get out of hand, he made it rain.

In this way, he deprived himself of the last sunrise. There was nothing but gray sky, misty, blowing, when he went out onto the riverbank that morning. But he did not really mind. The fresh air and the rain on his face were all the good-bye he could have asked for. He was sitting on wet grass wondering the last thought— why in God's name don't more people here realize what a beautiful world this is?—when he heard a voice behind him.

The voice was deep and very firm.

"Citizen Jell," it said.

The old man sighed.

"Coming," he said, "coming."

• • •

Vocabulary words:
Find these words in the section, write the sentence they are used in, and write your own definition. If you are stuck, look it up in the dictionary, but still write a definition in your own words.

infestation
conveyor

Comprehension/extension questions:

What would be the repercussions of removing the pests from our ecosystems?

Why did Mr. Jell break the rules when he was leading such an idyllic life?

What would you do with a Box?

Citizen Jell, by Michael Shaara, Published August 1959

Michael Shaara was born in Jersey City, New Jersey in June 23, 1928 and died May 5, 1988. He published a number of science fiction stories in the 1950s, and a novel, The Herald, in 1981.

BREAK A LEG

By JIM HARMON
Illustrated by GAUGHAN

The man worth while couldn't be allowed
to smile... if he ever laughed at himself,
the entire ship and crew were as good as dead!

If there is anything I am afraid of, and there probably is, it is having a rookie Accident Prone, half-starved from the unemployment lines, aboard my spaceship. They are always so anxious to please. They remember what it is like to live in a rathole behind an apartment house furnace eating day-old bread and wilted vegetables, which doesn't compare favorably to the Admiralty-style staterooms and steak and caviar they draw down in the Exploration Service.

You may wonder why anybody should make things so pleasant for a grownup who can't walk a city block without tripping over his own feet and who has a very low life expectancy on Earth due to the automobiles they are constantly stepping in front of and the live wires they are fond of picking up so the street won't be littered.

The Admiralty, however, is a very thorough group of men. Before they open a planet to colonization or even fraternization, they insist on knowing just what they are up against.

Accident Prones can find out what is wrong with a planet as easily as falling off a log, which they will if there is one lonely tree on the whole world. A single pit of quicksand on a veritable Eden of a planet and a Prone will be knee-deep in it within an hour of blastdown. If an alien race will smile patronizingly on your heroic attempts at genocide, but be offended into a murderous religious frenzy if you blow your nose, you can take the long end of the odds that the Prone will almost immediately catch a cold.

All of this is properly recorded for the next expedition in the Admiralty files, and if it's any consolation, high officials and screen stars often visit you in the hospital.

Charlie Baxter was like all of the other Prones, only worse. Moran III was sort of an unofficial test for him and he wanted to make good. We had blasted down in the black of night and were waiting for daylight to begin our re-survey of the planet. It was Charlie's first assignment, so we had an easy one—just seeing if anything new had developed in the last fifty years.

Baxter's guard was doubled as soon as we set down, of course, and that made him fidgety. He had heard all the stories about how high the casualty rate was with Prones aboard spaceships and now he was beginning to get nervous.

Actually Charlie was safer in space than he would be back on Earth with all those cars and people. We could have told him how the Service practically never lost a Prone—they were too valuable and rare to lose—but we did not want him to stop worrying. The precautions we took to safeguard him, the armed men who went with him everywhere, the Accident Prone First Aid Kit with spare parts for him, blood, eyes, bone, nerves, arms, legs, and so forth, only emphasized to him the danger, not the rigidly secured safety.

We like it that way.

No one knows what causes an accident prone. The big insurance companies on Earth discovered them when they found out in the last part of the nineteenth century that ninety percent of the accidents were happening to a few percent of the people. They soon found out that these people were not malingering or trying to defraud anybody; they simply had accidents.

I suppose everything from psychology to extra-sensory perception has been used to explain or explain away prones. I have my own ideas. I think an accident prone is simply a super-genius with a super-doubt of himself.

I believe accident prones have a better system of calculation than a cybernetic machine. They can take *everything* into consideration—the humidity, their blood sugar, the expression on the other guy's face—and somewhere in the corners and attic of their brain they *infallibly* make the *right* choice in any given situation. Then, because they are incapable of trusting themselves, they do exactly the opposite.

I felt a little sorry for Charlie Baxter, but I was Captain of the *Hilliard* and my job was to keep him worried and trying. The worst thing that can happen is for a Prone to give up and let himself sink into the fate of being a Prone. He will wear the rut right down into a tomb.

Accident Prones have to stay worried and thinking, trying to break out of the jinx that traps them. Usually they come to discover this themselves, but by then, if they are real professionals with a career in the Service, they have framed the right attitude and they keep it.

Baxter was a novice and very much of an amateur at the game. He didn't like the scoring system, but he was attached to the equipment and didn't want to lose it.

His clumsiness back on Earth had cost him every decent job he ever had. He had come all the way down the line until he was rated eligible only for the position of Prone aboard a spaceship. He had been poor—hungry, cold, wet, poor—and now he had luxury of a kind almost no one had in our era. He was drunk with it, passionately in love with it. It would cease to be quite so important after a few years of regular food, clean clothes and a solid roof to keep out the rain. But right now I knew he would come precariously close to killing to keep it. Or to being killed.

He was ready to work.

I knocked politely on his hatch and straightened my tunic. I have always admired the men who can look starched in a uniform. Mine always seemed to wrinkle as soon as I put them around my raw-boned frame. Sometimes it is hard for me to keep a military appearance or manner. I got my commission during the Crisis ten years back, because of my work in the reserve unit that I created out of my employees in the glass works (glassware blown to order for laboratories).

Someone said something through the door and I went inside.

Bronoski looked at me over the top of his picture tape from where he lay on the sofa. No one else was in the compartment.

"Where is Baxter?" I asked the hulking guard. My eyes were on the sofa. My own bed pulled out of the wall and was considerably inferior to this, much less Baxter's bed in the next cabin. But then I am only a captain.

Bronoski swung his feet off the couch and stood more or less in what I might have taken for attention if I hadn't known him better. "Sidney and Elliot escorted him down to the men's room, Captain Jackson."

"You mean," I said very quietly, "that he isn't in his own bath?"

"No sir," Bronoski said wearily. "He told us it was out of order."

I stifled the gurgle of rage that came into my throat and motioned Bronoski to follow me. The engines on the *Hilliard* were more likely to be out of order than the plumbing in the Accident Prone's suite. No effort was spared to insure comfort for the key man in the whole crew.

One glance inside the compartment at the end of the corridor satisfied me. There wasn't a thing wrong with the plumbing, so Baxter must have had something in mind.

On a hunch of my own, I checked the supply lockers next to the airlock while Bronoski fired questions at my back. Three translator collars were missing. Baxter had left the spaceship and gone off into an alien night.

Elliot and Sidney, the guards, were absolutely prohibited from interfering in any way with a Prone's decisions. They merely had to follow him and give their lives to save his, if necessary.

I grabbed up a translator collar and tossed one to Bronoski. Then, just as we were getting into the airlock, I remembered something and ran back to the bridge.

The thick brown envelope I had left on my desk was gone. I had shown it to Baxter and informed him that he should study it when he felt so inclined. He had seemed bored with the idea then, but he had come back for the report before leaving the ship. The envelope contained the exploration survey on Moran III made some fifty years before.

I unlocked a desk drawer with my thumb print and drew out a duplicate of the report. I didn't have too much confidence in it and I hoped Charlie Baxter had less. Lots of things can change on a planet in fifty years, including its inhabitants.

• • •

Vocabulary words:
Find these words in the section, write the sentence they are used in, and write your own definition. If you are stuck, look it up in the dictionary, but still write a definition in your own words.

fraternization
veritable
cybernetic

Comprehension/extension questions:

What use did the Service put accident prones to?

• • •

Bronoski picked up Baxter's tracks and those of the two guards, Elliot and Sidney, with ultra-violet light. They were cold splotches of green fire against the rotting black peat of the jungle path. The whole dark, tangled mess smelled of sour mash, an intoxicating bourbon-type aroma.

I jogged along following the big man more by instinct than anything else, ruining my eyes in an effort to refresh my memory as to the contents of the survey report in the cheery little glow from my cigarette lighter.

The lighter was beginning to feel hot to my fingers and I started to worry about radiation leak, although they are supposed to be guaranteed perfectly shielded. I read that before the last exploration party had left, they had made the Moranite natives blood brothers. Then Bronoski knocked me down.

Actually he put his hands in the small of my back and shoved politely but firmly. Just the same, I went face down into the moist dirt fast enough.

I raised my head cautiously to see if Bronoski would shove it back down. He didn't.

I could see through the stringy, alcoholic grass fairly well and there were Baxter, Elliot and Sidney in the middle of a curious mob of aliens.

Charlie Baxter had got pretty thin on his starvation diet back on Earth. He had grown a slight pot belly on the good food he drew down as Prone, but he was a fairly nice-looking young fellow. He looked even better in the pale moonlight, mixed amber and chartreuse from the twin satellites, and in contrast to the rest of the group.

Elliot Charterson and Sidney Von Elderman were more or less type-cast as brawny, brainless bodyguards. Their friends described them as muscle-bound apes, but other people sometimes got insulting.

The natives were less formidable. They made the slight lump of fat Charlie had at his waist look positively indecent.

The natives were *skinny*. How skinny? Well, the only curves they had in their bodies were their bulging eyeballs. But just because they were thin didn't mean they were pushovers. Whips and garrotes aren't fat and these looked just as dangerous.

Whenever I see aliens who are so humanoid, I remember all that Sunday supplement stuff about the Galaxy being colonized sometime by one humanlike race and the Ten Lost Tribes and so forth.

They didn't give me much time to think about it just then. The natives looked unhappy—belligerently unhappy.

I began to shake and at the same time to assure myself that I didn't have anything to worry about, that the precious Accident Prone would come out of it alive. After all, Elliot and Sidney were there to protect him. They had machine guns, flame-throwers, atomic grenades, and some really potent weapons. They could handle the situation. I didn't have a thing to worry about.

So why couldn't I stop shaking?

Maybe it was the way the natives were slowly but deliberately forming a circle about Charlie and his bodyguards.

The clothing of the Moranites hadn't changed much, I noticed. That was understandable. They had a non-mechanical civilization with scattered colonies that it would take a terrestrial season to tour by animal cart.

An isolated culture like that couldn't change many of its customs. Then Charlie shouldn't have any trouble if he stuck to the findings on behavior in the report. Naturally, that meant by now he had discovered the fatal error.

The three men were just standing still, waiting for the aliens to make the first move. The natives looked just as worried as Charlie and his guards, but then that might have been their natural expression.

I jumped a little when the natives all began to talk at once. The mixture of sound was fed to me through my translator collar while the cybernetic unit back on board the spaceship tried decoding the words. It was too much of an overload and, infuriatingly, the sound was cut out altogether. I started to rip my collar off when the natives stopped screeching and a spokesman stepped forward.

The native slumped a little more than the others, as if he were more relaxed, and his eyes didn't goggle so much. He said, "We do not understand," and the translation came through fine.

Baxter swallowed and started forward to meet the alien halfway. His boot slipped on the wet scrub grass and I saw him do the desperate little dance to regain his balance that I had seen him make so many times; he could never stay on his feet.

Before he could perform his usual pratfall, Sidney and Elliot were at his sides, supporting him by his thin biceps. He glared at them and shrugged them off, informing them wordlessly that he would have regained his balance if they had given him half a chance.

"We do not understand," the native repeated. "Do you hold us in so much contempt as to claim *all* of us as your brothers?"

"All beings are brothers," Charlie said. "We were made blood brothers by your people and my people several hundred of your years ago."

Charlie's words were being translated into the native language, of course, but Bronoski's collars and mine switched them back into Terrestrial. I've read stories where explorers wearing translators couldn't understand each other, but that isn't the way it works. If you listen closely, you make out the words in your own language underneath, and if you pay very close attention, you can find minor semantic differences in the original words and the echo translated back from a native language.

I was trying to catch both versions from Charlie. I knew he was making a mistake and later I wanted to be sure I knew just what it was. Frankly, I would have used the blood-brother gambit myself. I had also read about it in the survey report, as I made a point of telling you. This just proves that Accident Prones haven't secured the franchise on mistakes. The difference is that I would have gone about it a lot more cautiously.

"Enough of this," the native said sharply. "Do you claim to be *my* brother?"

"Sure," Charlie said.

Dispassionately but automatically, the alien launched himself at the Prone's throat.

• • •

Vocabulary words:
Find these words in the section, write the sentence they are used in, and write your own definition. If you are stuck, look it up in the dictionary, but still write a definition in your own words.

brawny
garrotes
terrestrial

Comprehension/extension questions:

Why would the alien attack Charlie Baxter?

• • •

Charterson and Von Elderman instantly went into action. Elliot Charterson jumped to Charlie's assistance while Sidney Von Elderman swung around to protect Charlie from the rest of the crowd.

But the defense didn't work.

The other aliens didn't try to get to Baxter, but when they saw Elliot start to interfere with the two writhing opponents, they clawed him down into the grass. Sidney had been set to defend the Prone, not his fellow guard. They might have been all right if he had pulled a few off Elliot and let him get to work, except his training told him that the life of a guard did not matter a twit, but that a Prone must be defended. He started toward Charlie Baxter and was immediately pulled down by a spare dozen of the mob.

It all meant one thing to me. The reaction of the crowd had been spontaneous, not planned. That meant that the struggle between Charlie and the spokesman was a high order of single combat with which it was unholy, indecent and dastardly to interfere.

I could fairly hear Bronoski's steel muscles preparing for battle as he saw his two mammoth pals go down under the press of numbers. A bristle-covered bullet of skull rose out of the grass beside me and it was my turn to grind his face in the muck.

I had a nice little problem to contend with.

I knew the reason Baxter had slipped out at night to be the first to greet the aliens. He was determined to be useful and necessary without fouling things up. I suppose Charlie had never felt valuable to anyone before in his life, but at the same time it hurt him to think that he was valuable only because he was a misfit.

He had decided to take a positive approach. If he did things right, that would be as good proof of conditions as if he made the mistakes he was supposed to do. But he couldn't lick that doubt of himself that had been ground into him since birth and there he was, in trouble as always.

Now maybe Bronoski and I could get him out ourselves by a direct approach, but Charlie would probably lose all self-confidence and sink down into accepting himself as an Accident Prone, a purely passive state.

We couldn't have that. We had to have Charlie acting and thinking and therefore making mistakes whose bad examples we could profit by.

As I lay on my belly thinking, Charlie was putting up a pretty good fight with the stringy native. He got in a few good punches, which seemed to mystify the native, who apparently knew nothing of boxing. Naturally Charlie then began wrestling a trained and deadly wrestler instead of continuing to box him.

I grabbed Bronoski by his puffy ear and hissed some commands into it. He fumbled out a book of matches and lit one for me. By the tiny flicker of light, I began tearing apart my lighter.

I suppose you have played "tickling the dragon's tail" when you were a kid. I did. I guess all kids have. You know, worrying around two lumps of fissionable material and just keeping them from uniting and making a critical mass that will result in an explosion or lethal radiation. I caught my oldest boy doing it one day back on Earth and gave him a good tanning for it. Actually I thought it showed he had a lot of grit. Every real boy likes to tickle the dragon's tail.

Maybe I was a little old for it, but that's what I was doing there in the Moran III jungle.

I got the shield off my cigarette lighter and jerked out the dinky little damper rods for the pile and started easing the two little bricks toward each other with the point of my lead pencil.

I heard something that resembled a death rattle come from Charlie's throat as the fingers of the alien closed down on it and my hand twitched. A blooming light stabbed at my eyes and I flicked the lighter away from me.

The explosion was a dud.

It lit up the jungle for a radius of half a mile like a giant flashbulb, but it exploded only about ten times as loud as a pistol shot. The mass hadn't been slapped together hard enough or held long enough to do any real damage.

The natives weren't fools, though. They got out of there fast. I wished I could have gone with them. There was undoubtedly an unhealthy amount of radiation hanging around.

"Now!" I told Bronoski.

He ran into the clearing and found four bodies sprawled out: Charlie Baxter, his two guards and the native spokesman.

Charlie and the native were both technically unconscious, but they each had a stranglehold on each other, with Charlie getting the worst of it.

Bronoski pried the two of them apart.

While he roused Sidney and Elliot from their punch-drunk state, I examined Charlie. He had a nasty burn on his leg and two toes were gone. If there was an explosion anywhere around, he was bound to be in front of it.

He was abruptly choking and blinking watery eyes.

"You did it, Charlie," I lied. "You beat him fair and square."

Charlie was in bed for the next few days while his grafted toes grew on, but he didn't seem to mind.

We knew enough not to use the blood-brothers approach after fifty years and therefore it did not take us long to find out why we shouldn't.

The Moran III culture was isolated in small colonies, but we had forgotten that a generation of the intelligent life-forms was only three Earth months. It seems a waste at first thought, but all things are relative. The Crystopeds of New Lichtenstein, for instance, have a life span of twenty thousand Terrestrial years.

With so fast a turnover in Moran III individuals, there was bound to be a lot of variables introduced, resulting in change.

The idea that seemed to be in favor was the survival of the fittest. Since the natives were born in litters, with single births extremely rare, this concept was practiced from the first. Unless they were particularly cunning, the runts of the litter did not survive the first year and rarely more than one sibling ever saw adulthood.

Obviously, to claim to be a native's brother was to challenge him to a test of survival.

My men learned to call themselves Last Brother in the usual bragging preliminaries that preceded every encounter. We got pretty good results with that approach and learned a lot about the changes in customs in the half century. But finally one of the men—either Frank Peirmonte or Sidney Charterson, who both claim to be the one—thought of calling the crew a Family and right away we began hitting it off famously.

The Moranites figured we would kill each other off all except maybe one, whom they could handle themselves. They still had folk legends about the previous visit of Earthmen and they didn't trust us.

Charlie Baxter's original mistake had supplied us with the Rosetta Stone[9] we needed.

Doctor Selby told me Charlie could get up finally, so I went to his suite and shook hands with him as he still lay in bed.

I waited for the big moment when Charlie would be on his feet again and we could get on with the re-survey of the planet.

"Here goes," Charlie said and threw back his sheet.

He swung his legs around and tottered to his feet. He was a little weak, but he took a few steps and seemed to make it okay.

Then the inevitable happened. He snagged the edge of one of the Persian carpets on the bedroom floor with his big toe and started to fall.

Selby and I both dived forward to catch him, but instead of doing the arm-waving dance for balance that we were both used to, he seemed to go limp and he plopped on the floor like a wet fish.

Immediately he jumped to his feet, grinning. "I finally learned to go limp when I take a fall, sir. It took

---

[9] A key to translation

a lot of practice. I imagine I'll save some broken bones that way."

"Yes," I said uneasily. "You have been thinking about this quite a lot while you lay there, haven't you, Baxter?"

"Yes, sir. I see I've been fighting this thing too hard. I am an Accident Prone and I might as well accept it. Why not? I seem to always muddle through some way, like out there in the jungle, so why should I worry or feel *embarrassed? I know I can't change* it."

I was beginning to do some worrying of my own. Things weren't working out the way they should. We were supposed to see that Prones kept developing a certain amount of doomed self-confidence, but they couldn't be allowed to believe they were infallible Prones. A Prone's value lies in his active and constructive effort to do the right thing. If he merely accepts being a Prone, his accidents gain us nothing. We can't profit from mistakes that come about from resignation or laughing off blunders or, as in this case, conviction that he never got himself into anything he couldn't get himself out of.

"Doctor Selby, would you excuse us?" I asked.

The medic left with a bow and a surly expression. I turned to Baxter, rather wishing Selby could have stayed. It was a labor dispute and I was used to having a mediator present at bargaining sessions at my glassworks. But this was a military, not a civilian, spaceship.

"I have some facts of life to give you, Baxter," I told him. "It is your duty to *actively* fulfill your position.

You have to make decisions and plan courses of action. Do you figure on just walking around in that jungle until a tree falls on you?"

He sat down on the edge of the bed and examined the pattern in the carpet. "Not exactly, sir. But I get tired of people waiting for me to make a fool out of myself. I have a natural talent for—for *Creative Negativism*. That's it. And I should be able to exercise my talent with *dignity*."

"If you don't actively fulfill the obligations of a Prone, you aren't allowed the luxuries and privileges that go with the position. Do you think you would like to be without your armed guards to protect you every moment?"

"I can take care of myself, sir!"

I paused and came up with my best argument. "How would you like to live like an ordinary spaceman, without rare steaks and clean sheets? Because if you're not our Accident Prone, you're just another crew member, you know."

That one hurt him, but I saw I had put it to him as a challenge and he must have had some guilt feelings about accepting all that luxury for being nothing more than he was. "I could fulfill the duties of an ordinary spaceman, sir."

I snorted. "It takes skill and training, Baxter. Your papers entitle you to one position and one only anywhere—Accident Prone of a spaceship complement. If you refuse to do your duties in that post, you can only become a ward of the Galaxy."

His jaw line firmed. He had gone through a lot to keep from taking such abject charity. "Isn't there," he asked in a milder tone, "*any* other position I could serve in on this ship, sir?"

I studied his face a moment. "We had to blast off without an Assistant Pile Driver, j.g.. It keeps getting harder and harder to recruit an APD, j.g. I suppose it's those reports about the eventual fatalities due to radiation leak back there where they are stationed."

Baxter looked back at me steadily. "There are a lot of rumors about the high mortality rate among Accident Prones in space, too."

• • •

Vocabulary words:
Find these words in the section, write the sentence they are used in, and write your own definition. If you are stuck, look it up in the dictionary, but still write a definition in your own words.

fissionable
inevitable
infallible

Comprehension/extension questions:

What are the chances that Charlie can act as a regular crewman?

How would you deal with him deciding not to actively seek out accidents?

• • •

He was right. We had started the rumors. We wanted the Prones alert, active and scheming to stay alive. More beneficial accidents that way. Actually, most Prones died of old age in space, which is more than could be said of them on Earth, where they didn't have the kind of protection the Service gives them.

"Look here, Baxter, do you like your quarters on this ship?" I demanded.

"You mean this master bedroom, the private heated swimming pool, the tennis court, bowling alley and all? Yes, sir, I like it."

"The Assistant Pile Driver has a cot near the fuel tanks."

He gazed off over my left shoulder. "I had a bed behind the furnace back on Earth before the building I was working in burned down."

"You wouldn't like this one any better than the one before."

"But there I would have some chance of *advancement*. I don't want to be stuck in the rank of Accident Prone for life."

I stared at him in frank amazement. "Baxter, the only rank getting higher pay or more privileges than Prone is Grand Admiral of the Services, a position it would take you at least fifty years to reach if you had the luck and brains to make it, which you haven't."

"I had something more modest in mind, sir. Like being a captain."

He surely must have known how I lived in comparison to him, so I didn't bother to remind him. I said, "Have you ever seen a case of radiation poisoning?"

Baxter's jaw thrust forward. "It must be pretty bad—but it isn't as violent as being eaten by floating fungi or being swallowed in an earthquake on some airless satellite."

"No," I agreed, "it is much slower than any of those. It is unfortunate that we don't carry the necessary supplies to take care of Pile Drivers. Most of our medical supplies are in the Accident Prone First Aid Kit, for the exclusive use of the Prone. Have you ever taken a good look at that?"

Baxter shivered. "Yes, I've seen it. Several drums of blood, Type AB, my type. A half-dozen fresh-frozen assorted arms and legs, several rows of eyes, a hundred square feet of graftable skin, and a well-stocked tank of inner organs and a double-doored bank of nerve lengths. Impressive."

I smiled. "Sort of gives you a feeling of confidence and security, doesn't it? It would be unfortunate for anyone who had a great many accidents to be denied the supplies in that Kit, I should think. Of course, it is available only to those filling the position of Accident Prone and doing the work faithfully and according to orders.”

“Yes, sir,” Charlie mumbled.

“Selby is your personal physician, you realize,” I drove on. “He takes care of the rest of us only if he has time left over from you. Why, when I was having my two weeks in the summer as an Ensign, I had to lie for half an hour with a crushed foot while the doctor sprayed our Prone’s throat to guard against infection. Let me tell you, I was in quite a bit of pain.”

Charlie’s pale eyes narrowed as if he had just made a sudden discovery, perhaps about the relationship between us. “You don’t make as much money as I do, do you, sir? You don’t have a valet? And your bed folds into the bulkhead?”

I thought he was at last beginning to get it. “Yes,” I said.

He stood sharply to attention. “Request transfer to position of Assistant Pile Driver, j.g., sir.”

I barely halted a groan. He thought I resented him and was deliberately holding him down into the miserable overpaid, overfed job that was beneath him and the talents that so fitted him for the job.

“Request granted.”

He would learn.

He had better.

I started to sweat in a gush. He had *really* better.

I took him into the rear of the ship and showed him where he would sleep. In the oily gloom, he regarded the pad from an old acceleration couch fitted to two scratched and nicked aluminum pipes jury-rigged between two squat tanks containing water for the atomic pile used close to planets where the gravitational field interfered with the star-drive.

"Over here's what you have to keep an eye on, Baxter," I told him.

We walked past the dimly lighted rows of towering fuel lines and cables. Charlie tripped over the hump of a deck-level cable housing. His knee banged against the deck plates and he stood with an effort.

"Careful," I said. "Now that you have limited medical attention, don't break a leg."

Baxter rubbed his leg thoughtfully. "Funny. My grandfather used to be in show business. He told me that telling somebody to break a leg was wishing them good luck."

I cleared my throat. "It would seem in dubious taste, addressed to an accident prone. However, you have my best wishes. You realize that your salary as Prone of 11,000 credits a month and your pay of 23 credits a month as an APD, j.g., are suspended until the Admiralty rules on your case."

"Yes, sir. I realize that, sir."

I stopped him in front of the soiled red box that was the tension gauge. "If the electrical control of the drive somehow becomes broken, the interrupted circuit will show on the gauge. It is then the duty of the APD, j.g., to go through the small airlock and maintain manual control of the pile while at least one of the control circuits is repaired. The job rarely has to be done, but when it is, it is very often fatal."

Baxter only nodded. "I understand."

I doubted that he did.

After leaving Baxter on his first watch, I went to the mess hall and waited for him to show up. The men knew what to do when he came.

It was rather pleasant to sit there savoring the odors. At times, they still seem more like those of a chemical laboratory than a kitchen, but I have become so used to associating burning starch products, centrifuged tannic acid, and melting dextrose with food that I am almost immune to the aroma of Prone food like juicy, sizzling steak. Almost.

Charlie Baxter finally came through the hatch. He paused and seemed to shake off what he must have thought was some olfactory hallucination and started to sit down at the table with the rest of the men. He looked rather pleased. He had probably decided being Accident Prone had deprived him of much of the company he had every right to enjoy with his shipmates.

"Get out of here!" Frank Peirmonte yelled, jumping up from the other end of the oblong table.

"Why?" Baxter asked in astonishment.

"Baxter," I put in, "I'm afraid the men think they may catch radiation fever from a pile driver like you."

"Catch radiation fever?" he repeated. "Men have been exposed to atomics for hundreds of years. Surely you men must know any poisoning in one individual can't be transmitted to another like germs. I couldn't absorb enough radiation to be dangerous to you in simple proximity and still be alive. Don't you see that?"

At once, all of my crew at the table covered their faces with their arms.

"Don't look at us!" Bronoski screamed, his voice knifing toward the higher octaves.

Baxter gaped in a daze from one of us to the other. "What do you mean? Why shouldn't I look at you?"

"You've got The Eye! *All* pile drivers get it."

"But I have to eat," he objected. "I'm hungry. Really I am."

I swung around and exchanged a few words with Tan Eck, the cook, at the rear hatch. I took a steaming tray and went across the compartment, averting my face.

"You will have to forgive these superstitious spacemen," I apologized to Baxter. "You go right ahead and eat just outside the door. I won't mind a bit."

"Thanks," Baxter said, accepting the plate. He looked down at the white paste, black gum and cup of yellowish liquid fitted in the proper holes and slots, then up at me. "What is this stuff?"

"You don't have to look right at me!" I snapped. "It is standard spaceman's fare—re-reconstituted carbohydrates, protein and hot ground roasted soya. This is stuff we had left over on our plates from lunch, all set to go into the converter, but Tan Eck reprocessed it for you. It's what regulations specify for an APD, j.g."

Baxter opened his mouth and closed it hard. "Yes, sir. Thank you, sir."

He turned smartly to leave and I halted him with a palm up. "Baxter."

He turned. "Yes, sir?"

"We are moving to the other side of the continent to continue with the re-survey. I want to make it clear to you that you are absolutely forbidden to leave the ship. We can't spare the guards for your liabilities, now that you have thrown away your value."

"Yes, sir."

Even at the time, I was gratified by the sudden thoughtful narrowing of his eyes.

• • •

Vocabulary words:
Find these words in the section, write the sentence they are used in, and write your own definition. If you are stuck, look it up in the dictionary, but still write a definition in your own words.

acceleration
jury-rigged
proximity
gratified
Comprehension/extension questions:

Why did the captain tell Baxter not to leave the ship? What effect do you think it will have?

Are the spacemen really that superstitious or not? What makes you think this?

• • •

I wasn't surprised the next day when Bronoski reported that Charlie Baxter had taken a backpack—food, soap, blankets and so forth—and left the *Hilliard*. He was determined to prove that he wasn't merely Accident Prone and could get things done on his own.

"Charterson and Von Elderman are following him?" I asked.

Bronoski nodded his bullet-shaped head. "Like a hawk."

"The Bird can follow him like a hawk. I want them to follow him like men."

"They are as good at the job as I am," Bronoski reassured me.

"I think," I said quickly, "that I had better go down to Communications and follow Baxter myself."

The Bird was an electronic device. It looked like a local life-form that was actually a flying mammal. Inside the thing was a sensitive video camera and a self-propulsion unit.

The Bird homed in on Baxter's electroencephalograph waves.

The view on the screen in front of the lounging chairs was clear but monotonous.

Charlie made his way across the landscape, woods on this side of the continent, not jungle, without incident. He did fall down like a wet laundry bag every so often, but that, as you'd figure, amounted to traveling across country without incident. He'd have done the same on a smooth pavement.

I had a cigarette in my mouth, futilely pounding my pockets for the lighter I didn't have, when Charlie met the alien.

There was only one native this time, the same thin form, but more lightly clothed here. I shifted uneasily and hoped the two guards were close. There was only one this time, but it was useless to suppose Charlie could handle him himself.

"Greetings," Charlie said. "I am Big Brother of a new Family."

There was no sound equipment in the Bird, but the translator circuits in the control board read Baxter's lips and produced their sound patterns for us. They would also translate the native's language, but just then he wasn't saying anything.

He walked around the Prone leisurely, as if considering buying him.

Charlie shifted the straps of his pack. He hadn't been convinced of his own abilities enough to take along a gun or any other kind of weapon. He would be almost sure to kill himself with it.

Or would he?

I suddenly wondered if Charlie doubted himself enough to commit outright suicide. He had had plenty of close calls, yet he had always survived. If his goal was self-destruction, he surely would have reached it after this many opportunities.

I watched the screen intently.

Charlie thought he was alone there with a possibly hostile native. All he had to do was make one small slip and he would be dead. Yet, so far, he had followed the pattern we had used at the other colony exactly.

Instantly I realized that it *must* be a mistake to follow the other pattern with this second group of aliens, if Charlie Baxter did it.

At first I couldn't understand why the pattern should be wrong for this group if it was right for the first. They were close enough so that there must have been intercourse between them, and if customs were violently different, there would probably be a state of warfare between them and none was apparent.

I finally realized why warfare would be almost impossible and why the customs of the separated colonies might be extremely at odds.

The colonies were three months apart by fastest transportation, which was longer than a generation of the natives. No one could live long enough to reach a second colony, so each culture developed in isolation along entirely random lines.

I felt like yelling at Charlie. There was literally no way of telling how he might be offending and antagonizing this Moranite by treating him as we had learned to treat the others.

The alien finally spoke. "You are part of a—Family?"

Charlie nodded his head.

So did the native—he bobbed Charlie's head with a rock.

"Close in on 'em fast but gentle," I radioed the guards.

The native dragged Baxter's limp body through a nearby thicket and into a small clearing. Abruptly I saw they were up against the base of the nearest mountain. A bubbling, dancing stream twisted through brown and green rock and disappeared into a ridge of gray slate. It reappeared below the hill, steaming, obviously passing through an underground hot springs.

The alien had Charlie where he wanted him before we could move. He lashed him securely with stringy vine and, with him thrown over his shoulder, ran up the slate, which rumbled down ominously behind them. He tossed Charlie over a wide hole at the top of the ridge. Slate rained down into the hole. If the Prone hadn't snapped awake and made his body rigid, he would have tumbled into the hole at that moment.

"So you wake, Familyman," the native said. "How could you admit to being anything so immoral when you were alone? You surely did not think you could eat me without help from the others of your evil brothers!"

Charlie licked his lips and moved his eyes; that was about all he dared move. "You—don't approve of families?"

The native drew himself up to his full elongated height in the screen. "Like all good People, I was properly abandoned at birth and I proudly say I have never associated with others except for Mating and Trading."

I noticed abstractly that he finished moving his lips long before the translation was finished. He was using a very primitive language. I screwed the button nervously in my ear for Charterson and Von Elderman to report.

• • •

Vocabulary words:
Find these words in the section, write the sentence they are used in, and write your own definition. If you are stuck, look it up in the dictionary, but still write a definition in your own words.

electroencephalograph
futilely
antagonizing

Comprehension/extension questions:

Do you think we will still be smoking cigarettes in the future? Why is smoking included in so many of these stories?

Why did Charlie Baxter fail in his contact with the new aliens?

• • •

The alien looked at the rigid form of Baxter over the pit. "I suppose I should have some pity for you. You began your filthy practice too young to know better. But imagine! Combining with others of your kind to survive—at the expense of decent individuals like myself. Robbing us, eating us. The Finger of Fire will come soon and will destroy you. I have heard Familymen often try to aid one another. Perhaps others of your kind will die with you!"

He was gone long before the translation was finished, leaving Charlie Baxter arched across a pit that widened as the alien's descent disturbed more of the soft shale.

The native was out of sight. I realized his tribe would soon be extinct. The racial mind for the whole species seemed obsessed with survival by natural selection, but his tribe had gone off on the tangent of individualism, which was fine to some extent, but the Service had learned that a race couldn't survive without *some* degree of cooperation and this one's level of mating and trading did not seem sufficient.

"Captain Jackson!" Von Elderman's voice said in my ear. "We can't reach him! If we start up that hill, the soft shale is bound to shift and drop him right into that hole."

"I'll send Bronoski with a personal flyer immediately to make an air pickup," I said numbly.

It wasn't the guards' fault. Charlie hadn't seemed to be in any immediate danger and we don't kill intelligent life-forms without damned good reason—the kind of reason that stands up in court. But he was now stretched over what I was fairly certain was an active geyser— "The Finger of Fire," the native had called it, and had assured Charlie that it would kill him.

I dispatched Bronoski, but that was all I could do. I did not know when the geyser would spout. Maybe Bronoski would make it. Maybe he wouldn't.

I magnified the view from the useless little Bird and studied Charlie's face in the screen. If he lay there doing nothing, waiting for a miracle to happen, he was—I shuddered—cooked. He had to make an active decision.

If he didn't, he was almost sure to die.

But maybe that was what he wanted. Maybe accident prones really want to destroy themselves.

It was his bid.

Slate dropped off the rim of the hole into the pit and Charlie stiffened. More passive acceptance. But maybe I wasn't being fair. There wasn't much Charlie could do. There wasn't much else for him to do except give up.

But I noticed his eyes moving. They went up to the bubbling ribbon of water and down to the steaming stream below the ridge where it emerged. Charlie smiled. He had made a decision.

He folded his knees and dropped into the hole.

He had naturally made the wrong decision. Bronoski in the flying platform swung into position above the pit.

Charlie must have figured that he would be washed on through the hot springs and out into the shallow water below. He would be, but he would be boiled alive.

Only there are mistakes and mistakes, and sometimes mistakes aren't mistakes at all.

The geyser exploded, higher, faster and harder than it ever had before. And Charlie, half-drowned and half-or-more scalded, popped up and landed in the brush twenty feet away.

Bronoski fought for control of his flyer and finally made a fast pickup.

Doc Selby did a pretty good job with the First Aid Kit. Charlie's neck and collarbone were broken and over fifty percent of his skin had to be replaced. Still, it was lucky Charlie had that concentrated soap in his pack. Ever been to Earth National Park and seen Old Faithful? You know what happened—they use soap to get the geyser spouting when it's off schedule.

We haven't told Charlie that it was anything but an accident that Bronoski was so handy. And we let him tell us about the changed customs of the natives. He resumed his regular position of Accident Prone when he saw realistically that he would inevitably be doing the same work and that he might as well get paid for it.

I often wonder if it was a genuine mistake the way he dropped into the geyser. Certainly he would have died if it hadn't been for the soap concentrates. If he took that into consideration, though, it wasn't a mistake at all, but a wise choice.

A few days ago, when he was leaving my office—that is, the bridge—I saw Charlie slip and start to fall. He didn't give up and go limp. He gave his old dance of struggling to regain his balance. *Only this time he made it!*

I began sweating again.

After all the time, effort and money the Service puts into acquiring and training a Prone, I wonder if it is possible for one to beat his problem and cease to be an Accident Prone or even an accident prone.

This afternoon, I passed Charlie Baxter's swimming pool and saw him poised on his diving board. I waved and rather jauntily extended his grandfather's wish for good luck: "Break a leg."

Charlie grinned back at me. "Yes, sir."

But he didn't.

It would be very reassuring if he would.

• • •

Vocabulary words:
Find these words in the section, write the sentence they are used in, and write your own definition. If you are stuck, look it up in the dictionary, but still write a definition in your own words.

sufficient
dispatched

Comprehension/extension questions:

Describe the perfect Accident Prone for the captain/the service.

Break a Leg, by Jim Harmon, Published November 1957

Jim Harmon was born in Mount Carmel, Illinois on April 21, 1933 and died February 16, 2010. He wrote many short stories and essays in the 1950s-1960s and three novels (two in the 60s and on in 2007).

Did you enjoy this book? Reviews and recommendations are vital to making a book successful. Please leave a review at your favorite online book store or review site and share it with your friends.

Continue on for additional materials:
Discussion Questions for your class or book club
Extension Activities
Biography

More Workman Classic Schoolbooks, other classics, and suspense/young adult fiction books by P.D. Workman can be found at pdworkman.com

Sign up for my mailing list to be notified of new releases by Workman Classic Schoolbooks and P.D. Workman

Discussion Questions

1. What similarities do you see between various of the stories?
2. How are they different than today's science fiction stories? How are they the same?
3. What themes are explored?
4. How does the present differ from the vision of the future in these stories?
5. Discuss the use of heroes and anti-heroes in the stories.
6. Do the majority of the stories have a moral message? If so, what? What makes science fiction a good or bad medium to impart a moral message?

Extension activities

- Write a science fiction story of your own
- Research what science fiction authors were popular at the time these stories were written (1950s)
- Research technological advances that had occurred around the time these stories were written
- Read *Fahrenheit 451* or *I, Robot*
- Make a list of new technologies you believe will be developed in the future. Draw them and give them names!
- Watch some popular 1950s science fiction movies, such as *The Thing* and *The Day the Earth Stood Still*
- Read a newspaper, magazine, or blog and list scientific advances that would seem incredible in the 1950s
- Read graphic novels and compare the similarities between classic sci fi and modern superheroes, manga, etc.
- Go to the museum to view old technology such as early aircraft, transmitters, computers, etc.

- What do you think of the styles of black and white pictures illustrating these stories? Draw a scene from one of them.
- Study theories of time travel, space travel, or multiple dimensions
- How big is the solar system? The universe? How many habitable planets are there? How long would it take to travel to the nearest one?
- Write a newspaper set in the future
- Make a diorama or picture of another planet and its inhabitants
- Pick a major problem in today's society and propose a solution. What might some of the unintended consequences of this solution be?